Please return on or before the latest date above.
You can renew online at *www.kent.gov.uk/libs*
or by telephone 08458 247 200

CUSTOMER SERVICE EXCELLENCE

Libraries & Archives

Kent
County
Council

00884\DTP\RN\07.07   LIB 7

THE CRIMSON RAMBLERS

Ready to perform in Andy McKay's concert party on the pier pavilion at Westpool, *The Crimson Ramblers* face more than they imagine ... As they travel by train to Westpool and enter a dark tunnel, a mysterious packet is thrown into their compartment. Then their summer show becomes a focal point for murder, mystery and sudden death. There are many people anxious to get possession of the packet — who are they? And why are they ready to commit murder for it?

Books by Gerald Verner
in the Linford Mystery Library:

THE LAST WARNING
DENE OF THE SECRET SERVICE
THE NURSERY RHYME MURDERS
TERROR TOWER
THE CLEVERNESS OF MR. BUDD
THE SEVEN LAMPS
THEY WALK IN DARKNESS
THE HEEL OF ACHILLES
DEAD SECRET
MR. BUDD STEPS IN
THE RETURN OF MR. BUDD
MR. BUDD AGAIN
QUEER FACE

GERALD VERNER

THE CRIMSON RAMBLERS

Complete and Unabridged

LINFORD
Leicester

First published in Great Britain

First Linford Edition
published 2012

British Library CIP Data

Verner, Gerald.
  The Crimson Ramblers. - -
  (Linford mystery library)
  1. Detective and mystery stories.
  2. Large type books.
  I. Title II. Series
  823.9'12–dc23

  ISBN 978–1–4448–1187–2

Published by
F. A. Thorpe (Publishing)
Anstey, Leicestershire

Set by Words & Graphics Ltd.
Anstey, Leicestershire
Printed and bound in Great Britain by
T. J. International Ltd., Padstow, Cornwall

This book is printed on acid-free paper

1

The short red-haired man in the rather loud check suit came over with two cups of coffee to where the pretty blonde girl was sitting at a small table in a corner of the crowded buffet at Victoria Station.

'It's a slander on a self-respecting beverage to call it coffee, Sharon,' he remarked in a pronounced Scots accent, setting the cups carefully down on the table, 'but there ye are.'

'Thanks, Andy,' said the girl, laughing. 'What time do we get to Westpool?'

Andy McKay, owner and principal comedian of 'The Crimson Ramblers' Concert Party, booked to play a season at the popular and salubrious seaside resort, pulled up a chair and sat down in front of her.

'Five thirty-four,' he answered. 'It's a good train. Ye'll have time for a rest this evening so that ye can turn up fresh for rehearsal early in the morning.'

'I've never played Westpool before,' said Sharon Roy, sipping her coffee.

'It's a nice place,' remarked Andy. 'The people who go there for their holidays like to spend money on amusement.'

'It'll be nice being in one place for the whole season,' she said. 'I hate touring. Those long Sunday train journeys . . . ' She broke off and waved across the buffet. 'There's Vera and Billy. Vera!'

A dark girl, good-looking, except for a rather sulky expression, and a round-faced young man, came over to the table.

'Hello, Sharon. Good morning, Andy,' greeted Vera Lee.

'You sit down, Vera,' said the young man, dragging up two more chairs. 'I'll go and get some coffee.'

'I'd rather have tea,' said Vera.

'Ye willna notice the difference,' remarked Andy.

'Where are the others?' asked the dark girl as she folded a coat over her suitcase and sat down.

'Beryl and Tony are already on the train,' said Sharon. 'They promised to keep seats for the rest of us.'

'What about our new baritone?' inquired Vera.

'I havena seen him yet,' said Andy.

Vera frowned. The sulky look deepened round her mouth.

'I hope we don't get him in our compartment. I don't like him.'

'Talking about me, dear?' asked the round-faced young man, coming back with two full cups in time to catch the last part of her sentence.

'No,' answered Vera. 'Howard Gilbert.'

'Oh,' said Billy Dale, dropping into a chair beside her. 'Queer sort of a chap, isn't he?'

'He's a wee bit peculiar,' agreed Andy, 'but he's a good singer and he didna haggle over the terms of his contract.'

'That covers a multitude of sins, doesn't it, Andy?' said Sharon, laughing.

'I wouldna say a multitude,' answered Andy cautiously, 'but it goes a long way.'

'I think there's something very shifty about him,' declared Vera. 'He can't look you straight in the face.'

'You're just not his type, darling,' said Billy with a grin.

'I should hate to be,' retorted Vera. 'He probably strangles his girl friends when he's tired of them.'

'I must introduce him to some of mine!' said Billy.

A girl passed by their table at that moment on the way to the counter. She was a pretty girl, dressed in a neat black suit with a small hat of the same hue perched saucily on her red head. She looked nervous and ill-at-ease and gave them a rather frightened glance as she went by. Billy's roving eyes followed her across to the counter,

'Quite attractive,' he murmured.

'Wolf!' said Vera.

'She looks scared enough to be Red Riding-hood,' remarked Andy.

'You'd better go and engage her for your next pantomime,' grinned Billy, twisting round in his chair to get a better look at the girl in black. 'I wonder what makes her look so scared.'

'Maybe she's seen what they put in the sandwiches,' said Andy.

'If they run out of 'ham' there's always you,' said Billy rudely.

'Ye're a very good pianist, Billy,' retorted Andy, 'but as a comic . . . ' He left the sentence unfinished but pinched his nose expressively.

'I suppose,' said Vera, lighting a cigarette, 'that I'll have to spend the evening traipsing round Westpool looking for digs.'

'Haven't you fixed?' asked Sharon.

'Half the addresses I wrote to didn't trouble to answer and the rest were full up,' said Vera.

'You're going to have a job,' said Billy cheerfully. 'They say Westpool's packed out.'

Andy rubbed his hands happily.

'Aye, it looks like being a vurry profitable season,' he remarked.

'I suppose so long as we fill the Dome it doesn't matter if I have to sleep on the sands,' said Vera a little sharply.

'If we dinna fill the Dome we'll all be sleeping on the sands,' said Andy.

'My landlady may be able to find something, Vera,' said Sharon. 'We'll ask her.'

'We'd better be getting to the train,'

said Andy. 'Collect your props, boys an' girls.'

They got up and made their way out of the buffet and the red-haired girl in black with the frightened eyes watched them until they were out of sight.

* * *

The Westpool train was filling up. Beryl Cameron, standing at the door of one of the compartments, was looking anxiously along the platform. She was on the plump side but it was an attractive plumpness.

'Nobody else here yet, Beryl?' asked a man's voice behind her. She turned with a start.

'Tony!' she exclaimed. 'How did you get there?'

'Came in farther down the train and walked along the corridor,' he answered. 'They're leaving it rather late, aren't they?'

'Yes. I've had a dreadful job keeping these seats,' said Beryl, glancing back at the compartment behind her on the seats of which she had arranged a rather meagre distribution of luggage, coats, and other oddments. 'The train's getting very full.'

'Let's hope they're all going to Westpool,' said Anthony Wayne. 'You know, Andy ought to distribute throw-aways of the show on the train.'

'For heaven's sake don't suggest it, or he will,' said Beryl in alarm.

'Well, it's good business.'

'I wish sometimes, Andy would think a little less of business.'

'And more of you, eh?'

'That's not what I meant at all,' said Beryl in confusion.

'Oh, yes, it was.'

'Nonsense.'

He gave her a gentle pat on the shoulder.

'Keep on trying,' he said. 'One of these days you may be able to compete with the box-office.'

'Here come Sharon, Billy and Vera,' said Beryl. 'I can't see Andy anywhere . . .' She peered anxiously up the long plat-form. 'Sharon — Sharon! Where's Andy?'

'He'll be along in a minute,' called

Sharon. 'He's gone to buy a paper.'

'I must get one too,' said Tony.

'Get me one, there's a dear,' said Beryl. 'Pick one with the juiciest headlines. I love a bit of scandal on a Sunday.'

She was still scanning the platform.

'I'll bring a selection,' answered Wayne and hurried away.

Sharon, Billy and Vera entered the compartment.

'Which is my seat?' asked Sharon, looking round.

'You can have any one you like, except mine,' answered Beryl. 'The right-hand corner seat. I'll be back in a minute.'

'Not while the train is standing in the station,' said Billy, grinning.

'Get along with you,' retorted Beryl good-naturedly. 'I'm going to see if I can find Andy.'

They began to select their seats, putting suitcases and coats on the rack.

'I'm going to get some chocolates,' said Vera. 'I've just got time.'

'I adore chocolates,' said Sharon, 'but I daren't eat them. I should put on pounds.'

'Vera puts in pounds instead,' grinned Billy.

'I don't have to worry about my figure,' said Vera as a parting shot from the doorway.

'Better get yourself a saucer of milk, darling!' called Billy, but she didn't hear him.

Andy appeared from the corridor, his arms full of papers.

'Have you seen Beryl, Andy?' asked Sharon. 'She went to look for you.'

Andy nodded.

'Aye,' he said, 'I saw her — from behind a pile of luggage.'

'Poor Beryl,' said Sharon. 'You're awfully unkind to her. She adores the ground you walk on.'

'Well,' remarked Andy, settling himself comfortably. 'She can have it!'

The red-haired girl in black passed along the corridor, looking quickly in as she went by. Sharon caught sight of her and turned to Billy.

'There's your girl friend again, Billy. She must be looking for you.'

'I wish you meant it,' retorted Billy.

'Anyway, it's a bit of luck she's on the train.' He got up and went out into the corridor. 'I think I'll just stroll along and see which compartment she's in.'

'Vera said you were a wolf,' called Sharon, but he took no notice.

'He's only a sheep — in wolf's clothing,' grunted Andy.

'I believe he only does it to make Vera mad,' said Sharon, lighting a cigarette.

'Aye, she's silly. She shouldna show it.'

Anthony Wayne came back. He was laughing.

'Billy's at it again,' he said. 'I've just seen him stalking his prey. Remarkably pretty girl too, if she didn't look scared to death.'

'I wonder what she's so frightened about?' remarked Sharon thoughtfully.

'I've never known Billy to have that effect on 'em before,' said Tony.

'It's not Billy. She was looking like that when we first saw her — in the buffet . . . '

'Maybe she'll turn to Billy for comfort,' said Tony. He looked at his watch. 'We should be off in just over a minute.'

'Andy,' cried Sharon anxiously, 'you must go and find Beryl. She'll be left behind looking for you.'

Andy got up with a sigh.

'Aye, I suppose I'd better,' he said reluctantly. 'She's a good pianist!'

He hurried away.

★   ★   ★

The train pulled out of the station dead on time, and Andy had only just succeeded in finding Beryl and getting back to their compartment before the whistle blew. She had been still wandering round, as Sharon had predicted, looking for him. As a consequence they were both rather breathless and Andy not a little cross. By the time they had left the outskirts of London, however, he had recovered his usual good temper. Billy was still absent. He had not come back to the compartment after going off to follow the red-haired girl — a fact which had considerably annoyed Vera Lee and which she was at no pains to conceal. She sat staring out of the window and munching

11

chocolate, steadfastly refusing to join in the general conversation.

The train sped smoothly on. Through towns and villages, open country and wooded hillside; through long cuttings and sidings full of laden coal trucks; through deserted stations and stations where little groups of people waited, it reeled out the miles steadily behind it on its way to the coast.

Heralded by a piercing scream from the engine it plunged suddenly into a tunnel and Beryl gave a little cry.

'Oh,' she said.

'What's the matter?' asked Sharon.

'I can't stand tunnels,' said Beryl nervously. 'They always frightened me as a child.'

For some reason the lights had not come on and it was pitch dark. The queer musty smell of old steam, which is one of the less pleasant attributes of all railway tunnels began to filter from the corridor into the compartment. The roar of the train was deafening and almost drowned the sudden sharp cry that Sharon gave.

Something had suddenly caught her a violent and painful blow on the side of her face.

'What's the matter?' said Andy who was sitting beside her.

'Something hit me,' she explained. 'Something hard . . . '

'It must have fallen from the rack,' said Anthony Wayne, looking up, and at that moment the lights in the roof came on. Billy Dale came into the compartment from the corridor at almost the same instant.

'Oh,' said Sharon resentfully. 'It was you, was it?'

He stared at her.

'Me what?' he demanded.

'Playing silly tricks,' she answered. 'What did you throw at me?'

'Throw at you,' he said, looking puzzled. 'Have you gone nuts? I didn't throw anything.'

Tony was searching about on the floor and picked up a small packet.

'This must be what hit you, Sharon,' he said, holding it up.

It was about the size of a packet of twenty cigarettes, wrapped in brown paper and sealed.

'Where on earth did that come from?' demanded Sharon in surprise.

13

'Somebody must have thrown it from the corridor,' said Tony.

Sharon looked at Billy suspiciously.

'Are you sure it wasn't you?' she said.

'Cross my heart,' he answered. 'I'd only just come out of the toilet.'

'Hold on,' said Wayne, who had been examining the packet with interest. 'There's something written on this. Look here?' He pointed to a pencilled scrawl.

'What does it say — 'Love from an Admirer'?' asked Billy.

Tony read it slowly: 'Please keep this safely. Will call at Dome Pavilion for it. Do not open'.'

'Aha,' said Billy dramatically. 'The mystery of the sealed packet. See next week's thrilling instalment.'

'Shut up, Billy,' snapped Vera. She was looking at the packet in Tony's hand curiously. 'I wonder what's in it?'

'Let's open it and see,' said Beryl.

Wayne shook his head.

'We can't do that,' he said. 'It says don't open.'

'I'll bet it's a joke,' said Andy. 'One of the holiday-makers playing tricks.'

'Well, I don't see the point,' remarked Sharon. 'Where does the laugh come?'

Tony looked at the small packet and his face was serious.

'Perhaps there isn't one,' he said slowly.

'What do you mean?' asked Vera.

'Well, supposing the person this thing belongs to wanted to get rid of it — get it out of their possession for a time . . .'

'Why should they?' demanded Billy.

'I don't know.' Wayne shrugged his shoulders. 'Because they were afraid of something, perhaps.'

'That girl,' exclaimed Sharon suddenly. 'The girl in black . . .'

'The one Billy was following?'

'Yes. What happened to her, Billy?'

'I missed her somehow. The corridor was packed . . .'

'It might have been anybody,' said Tony. 'It's useless conjecturing.'

'You'll know who it was when they come to claim it,' said Andy.

Tony nodded.

'It'll be interesting to see who does come, won't it?'

A man, who unseen by any of them,

was listening intently outside, in the corridor, moved away.

Wayne put the little packet away in his breast pocket and by the time they reached Westpool the incident was almost forgotten. None of them had any premonition of the queer and rather horrible series of events which awaited them there and of which that incident had been but the prelude.

2

The Dome Pavilion at Westpool is typical of pier pavilions in general. It is sited at the beginning of the pier with an entrance gay with coloured flags and plastered over with posters bearing flamboyant announcements of the opening of 'Andy McKay's Crimson Ramblers'.

The first performance was the Monday matinée and it opened to a packed house, due to a large extent to a sudden downpour of rain, which had driven the holiday-makers off the sands to seek shelter.

'They seem to like us,' said Sharon to Andy, as she came off breathless from her dance number and met him in the passage, behind the small stage, where the dressing rooms were.

'Aye, it's a good house,' said Andy, his small eyes sparkling. 'If we keep it up it'll be a good season.'

Sharon went into her dressing room and Andy made his way up to the stage where a burst of laughter greeted his entrance.

The passage ran the whole length of the back of the Pavilion to the stage door at one end that opened on to the pier. The dressing rooms were on one side, and on the other — a blank wall — were stored the large wickerwork prop baskets containing the dresses and small properties used by the concert party.

A door, halfway along the passage, opened as Sharon closed her door, and a man looked out.

Howard Gilbert, the newcomer to the concert party, was a thickset man with a rather heavy face. He looked quickly up and down the empty passage and there was something furtive in his attitude — as furtive as when he had stood listening outside the compartment on the train when Anthony Wayne had been discussing the packet that had so surprisingly been thrown from the corridor by someone unknown.

After a second or two he went back into the dressing room and shut the door. From the stage came the sound of music

18

played on the two pianos by Billy Dale and Beryl Cameron and then the door at the end of the passage — the door that led out on to the pier — opened and a girl came hesitantly in.

It was the red-haired girl in black.

She stood for a moment just inside the door looking rather uncertainly about her. Then she began to walk slowly along the passage, pausing every now and again outside each of the dressing room doors. She had passed the door of Wayne's room when he came out and she turned in alarm.

'Oh,' she began nervously. 'Excuse me, but . . . '

'Are you looking for someone?' he asked.

She nodded.

'I — I've called for a small packet . . . '

'Was it you who threw it into our compartment?' inquired Tony.

'Yes,' she answered eagerly. 'Have you got it? Can I have it, please?'

'Well, it's not here . . . '

Her face dropped.

'Not here?'

'No, it's at my lodgings.'

'When can I have it?' she asked. 'I must have it back as soon as possible.'

'Can you come in during the evening show?'

'Yes, yes.'

'I'll bring it down with me.' He looked at her curiously. 'Why did you throw it into our compartment?'

'I — I was afraid,' she answered. 'I — I can't explain . . . '

'Afraid of what?' he demanded.

'Something . . . ' She breathed the word so that it was almost inaudible.

'Something — or someone?'

She looked quickly up and down the passage.

'I'll come back,' she said hurriedly. 'I — I can't stop. I'll come tonight. You won't forget to bring it?'

'I won't forget,' he said.

She gave him a brief smile and almost ran down the passage to the stage door. The next second she had gone and the door banged shut behind her.

Tony stared after her a wrinkle of perplexity between his brows. Then he turned and went up to the stage.

* * *

'Well,' Andy McKay came bustling into the room he shared with Billy and Tony, 'that's the first show over.'

He sat down in front of the cracked mirror and began to remove his makeup.

'I had a visitor during the show this afternoon,' remarked Tony.

Billy looked up with a grin from the basin where he was washing his hands.

'Don't tell me you've enslaved some beauteous damsel already?'

'Well, she was quite pretty,' admitted Wayne.

'Some people have all the luck,' sighed Billy. He reached for a towel and began to dry his hands.

'The only person I ever seem to enslave is Beryl,' said Andy.

'Poor old Beryl. She does chase you around, doesn't she?' said Billy. 'What was your girl like, Tony?'

'You've seen her,' said Tony. 'The red-haired girl in black — on the train — remember?'

Billy threw down the towel and picked up his tie.

'Did she come to claim the packet?' he asked.

Tony nodded.

'Did ye give it to her?' asked Andy.

'I haven't got it here.'

'So it was she who threw it into our compartment,' grunted Billy. 'Just my luck that I wasn't around when she came.'

'She's coming back this evening,' said Tony, reaching for his shirt.

'I'm stuck to that confounded piano all through the show.' Billy made a grimace at himself in the mirror. 'Did she say why she got rid of the packet on us?'

'She admitted that she was afraid . . . '

'Of what?' put in Andy.

Tony shook his head.

'She didn't say.'

'It's a jolly queer business altogether,' said Billy.

'Sharon was right — about the girl,' said Andy.

'I wonder,' murmured Tony thoughtfully.

'Well, of course she was,' said Billy in surprise. 'The girl came to claim the packet, didn't she?'

'Anybody can claim anything,' said

Tony. 'If you don't know who the rightful owner is.'

'Aye, I see what you mean,' said Andy. He went over to the basin and began washing.

'For all I know,' Tony went on, 'she may be quite genuine. But, as you said just now, it's a jolly queer business. Did she get rid of the packet because she was afraid someone would try and take it from her? Or did somebody else get rid of it because they were afraid she was after it? See what I mean?'

'Are you going to give it to her?' asked Billy.

'She'll have to do a little explaining first. I've an idea that this packet business is tied up with something much bigger.'

'Ye've been reading too many detective stories,' said Andy raising a dripping face from the basin and groping for his towel. 'Ye'll probably find it's simple enough.'

'I expect you're right, Andy,' said Tony. 'But I'm curious.'

'You know what happened to the cat that was curious?' said Billy. 'I'm going to get some tea — at the café on the front, if

I can get in. I wonder what the girls are going to do?'

It appeared that they all had the same idea.

'What about you, Andy?' asked Beryl. 'Are you coming?'

Andy shook his head.

'I'm going round to the box office to see what the bookings are like,' he said hastily.

'The bookings! He dreams about them!' wailed Beryl.

When they had all gone laughing and joking out the stage door, Howard Gilbert came cautiously out of his dressing room. He waited for a little while to make sure that they had gone and then he went to the stage door and opened it. He uttered a soft whistle and a short, thin little man slipped quickly inside.

'Be careful,' whispered Gilbert, 'McKay's about somewhere.'

'Somethin' went wrong,' muttered the little man.

'I know,' said Gilbert. 'Come into my dressing room.'

The evening performance of 'The Crimson Ramblers' was nearing its end. Sharon, coming down from the stage for a quick change, ran into Tony in the passage.

'Has the girl been yet?' she asked.

'No — not yet,' he answered.

'The show's nearly over . . . '

'Perhaps she's in front,' he said. 'She'll come round after, I expect.'

She nodded and hurried on into her dressing room. Tony went on up to the stage. When he had finished his number with Vera he came back to his dressing room and sat down to enjoy a cigarette until he would be wanted for the finalé. Andy came in.

'Ye've no got rid of the packet yet?' he asked.

'No, she hasn't turned up.'

'Curious. I thought she was anxious to get it back,' said Andy.

'She was . . . '

'Ah, weel, there's time yet,' said Andy, looking at himself in the mirror and making a dab here and there at his makeup. 'Did she no say what her name was?'

'No, she was off like a startled rabbit when she found I hadn't got the packet here.'

There was a gentle tap at the dressing-room door.

'Here she is now,' said Andy and called: 'Come in. But it was not the red-haired girl in black who entered. It was a very large, enormously fat man, with jowls that hung down on either side of his face in flabby lumps of flesh. His small, beady eyes were sunk deeply in rolls of fat and Wayne thought he had never seen such an altogether unpleasant-looking person.

'Excuse me,' said the newcomer in a high-pitched voice, 'Do I intrude?'

'Aye, ye do! What do you want?' said Andy.

The fat man laughed. It was a jerky, spasmodic laugh, without mirth behind it.

'My niece was to have called this evening, sir,' he said. 'To collect a small packet . . . '

Tony stared at him.

'Your niece?' he repeated.

The fat man inclined his head.

'My niece, sir. Unfortunately she has been detained and has sent me in her stead. Perhaps you would be good enough to inform me, sir, to whom I apply?'

'Nothing doing,' said Tony.

The fat man raised his eyebrows.

'I beg your pardon, sir?'

'The packet you mention is in my possession,' said Tony, 'but I have no intention of parting with it except to its rightful owner.'

'But, my dear sir, I am its rightful owner,' asserted the fat man. 'My niece was merely acting on my behalf.'

'Look here, Mr. — Mr. — ' began Tony.

'My name is Beatal, sir — Simon Beatal.'

'We've a lot of your relations in the Dome,' said Andy.

Simon Beatal turned towards him.

'I fail to comprehend, sir,' he said.

'Black ones,' said Andy with a chuckle. 'Ye're a vurry prolific family.'

For a moment there was a flash of rage in the small blackcurranty eyes. But it was gone in a second and was replaced with jerky laughter.

'You are pleased to joke, sir,' said Simon Beatal.

'I'm not at all sure, Mr. Beatal,' said Tony, 'that even your niece is the rightful owner. The packet came into my possession in rather peculiar circumstances.'

'The foolishness of an imaginative and highly strung girl, sir,' explained Simon Beatal smoothly. Nothing more, I assure you. The contents of the packet are of a certain value. My niece received the impression on the train — purely mistaken, I am convinced — that she was being followed. There was a man who seemed to be watching her very closely, whom she described as of a criminal type. No doubt he was merely interested in her physical attractions. There are, I believe, such men, sir. In a sudden panic she . . . Well, you know what she did, sir.'

Tony shook his head.

'That's just it, I don't,' he said obstinately. Anybody could have thrown that packet into our compartment.

The expression on Simon Beatal's face hardened. His eyes were like two little black pebbles.

'Come, come, sir,' he said impatiently. 'I respect your scruples. But don't carry them too far. That packet is mine and I must request you to give it me.'

'If you want it you'll have to call at the nearest police station,' said Tony.

Simon Beatal was startled.

'Police station, sir?' he echoed.

'I'm taking it round there as soon as the show's over,' said Tony. 'I intended to tell your niece the same, if she'd turned up.'

The expression of the fat man's face was malignant.

'I warn you, sir,' he almost snarled, 'that I am not the sort of man to be trifled with.'

'I'm not trifling,' retorted Tony briefly.

'We'll be late for the finalé,' broke in Andy searching among the litter on the dressing table.

'Ye'll have to go, Mr. Slug . . . '

'Beatal, sir.'

'Aye I knew it was something that crawled. Where did I put that big prop cigar. The one that lights up at the end.'

'I haven't seen it, Andy,' said Tony.

'I'll have to get a spare one out of the prop basket,' cried Andy. He rushed over to the door. 'Come on!'

'Your friend is facetious, sir,' said Simon Beatal, 'but I assure you there is nothing humorous in this matter.'

'I'm inclined to agree with you,' answered Tony grimly.

'If I could persuade you to listen to reason, sir . . . '

'I've no time to listen to anything,' snapped Tony.

There was a sudden sharp cry from the passage outside as he opened the door. Andy, his face strained even beneath the makeup, was staring into one of the big prop baskets.

'Tony . . . Tony . . . For God's sake come here,' he called in a horrified voice. 'Come here — quickly . . . '

'What's the matter?' Tony hurried over to his side.

'Look . . . ' Andy stabbed a finger at the interior of the basket and Tony looked.

In it lay the red-haired girl in black.

'She's dead,' whispered Andy huskily. 'She's been strangled . . . '

3

From the direction of the stage came a burst of applause and then the two pianos began a catchy melody.

Andy dropped the lid of the basket, shutting out the horrible sight.

'That's the finalé,' he cried. 'Come on. We'll be off . . . '

'But, Andy . . . ' began Tony. But Andy wasn't listening. He gripped Tony by the arm and pulled him away up the passage.

Simon Beatal stood watching them until they were out of sight and then he went over to the basket and raised the lid . . .

★　★　★

'What was the matter?' asked Sharon as they all came trooping down from the stage after the finalé. 'You two were nearly off . . . '

'Yes, what's up, Andy?' asked Billy. 'You

and Tony look all dithery.'

Tony pressed his arm.

'Shut up,' he whispered.

'Sharon and I are going to the fun-fair,' said Vera. 'Coming, Billy?'

'Rather, I like fun-fairs,' said Billy.

'You and Tony coming, Andy?' asked Sharon.

'We'll no be able to,' answered Andy. 'We've some vurry important business to attend to.'

'Don't you ever relax, Andy?' said Beryl.

'I can't relax at the moment,' said Andy. He almost dragged Tony into their dressing room and shut the door.

'We ought to get hold of the police, Andy,' said Tony. 'There will be trouble if we don't . . . '

'Aye,' agreed Andy. 'I didna want to say anything before the . . . '

Billy came in quickly.

'Now look here,' he said. 'What's it all about? What's up?'

'It's the girl,' explained Tony. 'The girl in black . . . '

'What about her?' demanded Billy.

Tony told him.

'Good Heavens!' exclaimed Billy when he had finished. 'This is horrible. Strangled . . . in the prop basket . . . I say,' he added suspiciously. 'You're not pulling my leg, are you?'

'Go and look for yourself,' said Andy. He opened the door and they all went out into the passage. The rest of the company were changing and it was deserted.

Andy pointed to the basket.

'There ye are,' he said.

Billy went over to the basket and raised the lid.

The next moment he had dropped it with a hoot of laughter.

'You didn't expect to take me in with that, did you?' he said. 'For a moment I really believed you . . . '

'Do ye mind the waxworks — opposite the stage door?' said Andy. 'There was the figure of a girl outside the booth to advertise the show.'

'A girl in a summer frock,' said Tony.

'Aye,' agreed Andy. 'Well. That's it — in the basket.'

'Why did he do it?' asked Billy. 'It must have been risky?'

'It was worth it,' answered Tony grimly. 'It ties our hands completely. What d'you suppose the police 'ud say if we went to them now with our story of a strangled girl in a basket? And then showed them that dummy.'

'They'd no believe a word of it,' said Andy.

'Exactly. That was the idea,' said Tony.

'But he couldn't have carried the real body off the pier . . . ' began Billy.

'He didn't have to,' interrupted Tony. 'There's a high tide.'

They looked at each other, and Billy gave a little shiver.

In the dressing room next door, Howard Gilbert was examining a small black hat. Attached to it was a long red hair. He removed the hair carefully, opened a large travelling trunk, put the hat inside and locked the trunk. He looked worried and anxious as he began to remove his makeup.

'Look here,' said Billy, putting on his jacket. 'I just can't believe all this, you know. You two must have made a mistake.'

'There was no mistake,' said Andy emphatically. 'Besides the dead girl in the basket didna have the same dress on as that dummy. She was dressed in black!'

'But,' persisted Billy, 'who killed her, *when* did they kill her, and how did she *get* in the basket?'

'How do I know?' retorted Tony impatiently. 'She *was* there, that's all I know.'

'Perhaps she wasn't dead . . . '

'She was,' said Andy. 'She had a scarf tied tightly round her neck.'

'She might not have been dead,' argued Billy. 'She may have recovered and walked away herself.'

'What do you suppose she was doing in the basket at all?' asked Tony sarcastically. 'Playing hide and seek?'

'Well, you may not be so far out, eh?' said Billy. 'She was scared, wasn't she? She may have been hiding from somebody. This fat chap, what's-his-name . . . '

'How do you know he was fat?' asked Tony quickly.

Billy looked a little confused.

'You told me — or else it was Andy,' he said.

There was a tap at the door and Vera's voice called:

'We're ready, Billy.'

'Coming now, darling,' cried Billy. 'Good night, you chaps. See you tomorrow.'

'Don't say anything to the girls,' warned Andy.

'Don't worry,' answered Billy with a grin. 'Your deadly secret is safe with me.'

He went out with a wave of his hand.

'He doesna believe a word of it,' grunted Andy.

'Queer he should describe Beatal as a fat man,' muttered Tony thoughtfully. 'Neither of us mentioned it.'

'I don't like it, Tony,' said Andy very seriously. 'I don't like it at all. I canna get the sight of that poor wee girl out of my mind. I didna make any mistake about her.'

'Neither did I,' said Tony.

'That packet's at the bottom of it,' said Andy. 'The sooner ye get rid of it the better.'

'I'll turn it over to the police first thing in the morning,' said Tony.

'I wouldna wait. Do it tonight.'

'Perhaps you're right.' Tony went over to the suitcase in which he had put the little packet and opened it.

The packet had gone.

★ ★ ★

There was a rehearsal on the following morning. Sharon was putting in a new number for the following week and Andy was making several slight alterations to the programme.

'It was no too bad for a first run through,' he remarked as they left the stage. 'It'll work up fine.'

'I can put a lot more in it yet,' said Sharon.

'Ye'd find it better if Billy and Beryl could take the tempo a wee bit faster . . .'

'That's easy,' said Billy.

'I felt that's what it wanted,' agreed Beryl.

'I suppose,' said Vera cattily, 'if Andy had said it was too slow, you'd have felt that too?'

'It would be better faster,' said Sharon

hastily. 'Give it more pep.'

'Anything more, Andy?' asked Vera.

He shook his head.

'No, ye can all go away and enjoy yourselves until the matinée.'

They trouped out of the dark passage into the sunshine of the pier. Vera and Billy elected to go for a swim. Andy, as usual, and to the disappointment of the hopeful Beryl, went off to do some accounts. Tony and Sharon decided that coffee would be nice and went off together to find a café.

They found one on the front that was not too crowded and settled themselves at a corner table. There was a vacant table nearby and they had scarcely taken their seats when the little, thin-faced man, who had spoken to Gilbert, followed them in and sat down at the vacant table. He pulled out a newspaper and became engrossed in its contents, holding it so that he was screened from their view.

'I've been waiting for a chance to talk to you, Tony,' said Sharon, when the waitress had brought the coffee. 'What really happened last night?'

'What happened?' repeated Tony innocently.

'Don't look vacuous. Something happened. You know it did. When you and Andy came on for the finalé you both looked scared to death. As if you'd seen a ghost.'

'Imagination,' he declared.

She shook her head.

'No, it wasn't. Had it anything to do with that girl and the packet?'

'What makes you think that?'

'I just wondered. Did she come back for it?'

'No,' he answered truthfully, 'she didn't.'

'You're hedging,' she accused. 'Something did happen and it was to do with that girl and the packet . . .'

A shadow fell across the table — a huge distorted shadow that blotted out the ray of sunlight from the wide window. Sharon drew in her breath sharply and looked up.

'We meet again, Mr. Wayne,' said Simon Beatal. 'It is indeed a pleasant surprise.'

'For which of us?' said Tony.

'For both of us, I hope, sir. You permit me to sit down?' Without waiting for a reply he drew up a chair and lowered his huge body into it. 'I trust you will forgive me for my somewhat hasty departure last night — a business appointment, sir. Punctuality is one of my virtues. You and your friend found out your little mistake?'

He uttered one of his little mirthless, jerky laughs.

'Was it a mistake?' asked Tony.

'A stupid trick, sir.' Beatal laughed again. 'A practical joke played by someone with a childish sense of humour.'

'So you looked, did you?' said Tony.

'Naturally, sir. I was greatly relieved . . . '

'I hope your niece is well,' said Tony.

'In the best of health, sir,' said Simon Beatal. 'I trust you have reconsidered your attitude, Mr. Wayne?'

'About what?' asked Tony.

'You are cautious, sir. An excellent trait — if it is not carried to extremes.'

'Meaning?'

'You are an intelligent man, sir. It will be to your own interests to grant my previous request. You are dabbling in dangerous matters, sir.'

'I'm beginning to believe you,' said Tony grimly.

'I'm glad to hear it. Perhaps it will alter your outlook, sir.'

'But not, I'm afraid,' said Tony, 'to your advantage, Mr. Beatal.'

'That is a pity, sir,' replied Simon Beatal. 'You may, indeed, find it a great pity.'

'Is that a threat?' demanded Tony.

'A threat, sir?' Beatal uttered another of his jerky little laughs. 'Nothing so melodramatic — just a friendly warning, sir.'

'I'm afraid you are wasting your time,' said Tony shortly.

'I never waste anything, sir.'

'What you want is no longer in my possession.'

The suaveness vanished from Simon Beatal's face as though a sponge had been drawn across it. For a moment he looked like an enraged demon.

'What have you done with it? Where is it?' he demanded harshly.

'Wasn't it you who took it from my

dressing room last night?' asked Tony.

The fat man recovered his usual smooth attitude.

'If you are bluffing, sir,' he said, 'I should advise you to change your mind. If it is a question of money . . . '

'It isn't.'

'Then what is it you want? I am prepared to give you anything within reason, sir.'

'Can't you understand plain English, Mr. Beatal?' said Tony. 'I no longer have the packet. Is that clear?'

'I hear what you say, sir.' Simon Beatal got up. 'I apologise for my intrusion, sir. You have not seen fit to introduce me to your charming companion — ' he bowed to Sharon ' — an oversight that can be rectified in the future, sir. I have a feeling that we shall meet again. Let me offer you a word of advice, Mr. Wayne. Keep out of this business.' He laughed. 'You see I am generous. In spite of your refusal to cooperate I bear you no malice. Good day, sir.'

He bowed again to Sharon and made his way out of the café. The little man behind the newspaper got up quietly, folded his paper, and went after him.

Sharon gave a shiver.

'Who is that horrible man, Tony?' she asked.

'He calls himself Simon Beatal,' answered Tony.

She shivered again.

'He's horrible — he frightens me . . . Let's go Tony. Let's get out into the sunshine.'

4

The small, thin-faced man opened the stage door and looked cautiously into the passage beyond. It was empty and he could hear the sound of the show in progress, for the matinée was half over. Very stealthily he entered and made his way along to Howard Gilbert's dressing room. He tapped on the door.

Gilbert opened it quickly and frowned as he saw who had knocked.

'I told you not to come here,' he muttered angrily.

'It's urgent,' said the little man.

'All right. Come in.' Gilbert almost dragged him into the room and shut the door.

Sharon came out of her dressing room almost at the same moment. If she had been a second sooner she would have seen the little man go into Gilbert's room but she had no knowledge of his presence. She went quickly along towards the stage and ran into Tony as he came down the steps. From inside the theatre came a howl of laughter.

'Andy's going well this afternoon,' she said.

The whole show's going well,' said Tony. 'There's something the matter with Vera, though . . .'

'I know,' Sharon frowned. 'She's awfully touchy lately. You have to be careful what you say or she bites your head off.'

'She always was on the catty side,' said Tony.

'She's got worse lately. Do you think something's worrying her?'

'It's Billy probably,' said Tony. 'She's nuts about him and he's always dithering around after other girls.'

'I don't think it's entirely that.'

'What do you think it is?' He smiled down at her. 'A guilty secret?'

'What made you say that?' she asked quickly.

'I was only joking. You didn't think I was serious, did you?'

'No, but that's exactly how she's behaving.'

'I wouldn't worry, if I were you,' he said.

'I'm not worrying,' said Sharon. 'But with all these queer things going on . . . the packet and that frightened girl . . . and that horrible fat man . . . '

'The ubiquitous Mr. Beatal?' Tony smiled.

'Yes, and then there's you and Andy . . . '

'What's wrong with us?'

'There's something going on between you. It's no use pretending . . . Something happened last night. What did that man mean about a practical joke?'

'The less you know about it the better,' said Tony seriously.

'So there is something?' she said quickly. 'Why did he warn you to keep out of it?'

There was a burst of applause from the direction of the stage.

'That's the end of Andy's act,' said Tony. 'You'd better hurry or you'll be off.'

'You're not getting out of it as easily as that,' said Sharon. 'I'll see you later.'

She hurried up the steps to the stage. Tony looked after her and then made his way to his dressing room. He lit a cigarette and sat down smoking thoughtfully.

Howard Gilbert looked at the thin-faced little man perched on a corner of his dressing table and there was a worried frown on his heavy face.

'When did they find it?' he asked.

'A few minutes ago,' answered the other. 'I thought I'd better come and tell you at once.'

'Go back and get hold of all the information you can,' said Gilbert. 'I'll meet you after the show. Outside the café opposite the pier.'

'Okay, I'll do me best.'

'And be careful,' warned Gilbert. 'Be very careful.'

'You can trust me,' said the little man. He went over to the door.

'Wait,' said Gilbert. He opened the door and looked out. 'The coast's clear. Hurry, I don't want anyone to see you.'

The little man nodded and hurried away.

Gilbert watched him until he had shut the stage door behind him and then he came back into the dressing room. For a moment he stood thoughtfully looking at himself in the mirror and then he went over to the large trunk, unlocked it and took out the small black hat. He found a sheet of brown paper that had had laundry in it and very carefully made the hat into a parcel.

Putting it down on the dressing table he sat and stared at it as though trying to make up his mind . . .

★   ★   ★

Andy came hurriedly into the dressing room and began to change.

'That woman,' he declared, 'is becoming a menace!'

'Which woman?' asked Tony.

'There's only one woman in my life,' said Andy.

'What's she been up to now?'

'She wants to take me out to tea. She was nearly in tears when I said I hadna got the time. She even offered to pay the bill as an inducement!'

'What could be fairer than that?' said Tony laughing. 'You'll have to do one of two things, Andy sack her or marry her.'

'She's a contract for the season. It would be cheaper to marry her!'

'You might do worse.'

'Aye — I could fall off the end of the pier and drown, maybe!'

'I think Beryl would make a very good wife.'

'We'll drop the subject, if ye dinna mind,' said Andy firmly. 'Have ye seen anything more of Beatal?'

Tony told him about the morning meeting.

'But I thought he was the one who took the packet from your suitcase,' commented Andy.

'So did I,' agreed Tony. 'We were both wrong apparently.'

'If he didna take it who did?'

'Don't ask me.' Tony shrugged his shoulders.

'I wonder what's in it to make it so valuable?'

'I rather wish I'd looked now,' said Tony.

'Maybe it's just as well ye didn't,' said Andy meaningfully.

'You mean it might have proved dangerous?'

'Aye. Ye mind what happened to that girl?'

'We've no proof that anything happened to her. I agree with you that Beatal would stop at very little to get hold of the thing. He offered to bribe me to give it to him and I don't think he meant chicken feed. The contents of that packet are worth money — big money, Andy.'

'It's better out of your hands, in my opinion,' remarked Andy.

'Maybe you're right. I'd like to know, though, what . . . ' Tony broke off as Sharon came bursting excitedly into the room.

'Tony — Andy!' she cried. 'They've found the dead body of a woman — in the sea — at the end of the pier . . . '

'When?' asked Tony quickly.

'This afternoon — while the show was on.' She was breathless. 'Ted, the electrician, has just told me. One of the fishermen's lines caught in it.'

Andy shot a quick glance at Tony.

'The girl in the basket,' he murmured.

'What girl — what basket?' demanded Sharon.

'Was the woman drowned?' asked Tony. 'The woman they found?'

'I suppose so — I don't know,' she answered. 'The police have cleared the end of the pier and are keeping everybody away . . . You know something about it, don't you?' she accused. 'You and Andy. It's got something to do with what happened last night . . . Tony! Is it that girl — the girl in black?'

'Ye'll do well to keep out of it, Sharon,' said Andy.

'That's what that horrible man said this morning. He warned Tony . . . '

'It was good advice, I'm thinking,' said Andy seriously. 'There's something going on that we don't understand and maybe it's as well that we don't. Our job is to entertain the public and we don't want to get mixed up with murder . . . '

Sharon looked at him with horrified eyes.

'Murder?' she gasped. 'Do you mean that the woman they found was murdered?'

'I wouldna know.' Andy shook his head. 'But it's not our affair.'

Vera Lee, her face worried and anxious, came quickly into the room.

'Andy,' she said in an agitated voice, 'there's a man wants to see you. He says he's a police inspector . . . '

'Superintendent, miss,' interrupted a voice behind her and a big man followed her into the room. 'Are you Mr. McKay, sir?'

'Aye, that's my name,' said Andy.

'Sorry to bother you, sir,' said the big man. 'I'm Superintendent Halliday of the Westpool Criminal Investigation Department. We're inquiring into the death of a woman whose body was taken out of the sea this afternoon.'

'Drowned?' interpolated Tony.

'No, sir, strangled — with a silk scarf that was still knotted round her neck,' said Halliday. 'It's a pretty obvious case of murder.'

'Why have ye come to me?' asked Andy.

'We're trying to identify the woman, sir,' said Halliday. The body had got wedged in the piles under the pier . . . It's not a very pleasant thing to talk about but, well, the battering of the sea . . . '

Sharon went a little white and Vera put up her hand quickly to her mouth. They could imagine what the Superintendent had left unsaid.

'I still don't see how I can help ye,' said Andy.

'It seems you may have known the woman, sir,' answered Halliday. 'She was wearing a black suit and we found a bit of paper in one of the pockets with your name on it. The paper was very sodden but just decipherable.'

'What colour is her hair?' asked Sharon before she could stop herself. The Superintendent turned to her in surprise.

'Reddish, miss,' he said. 'Auburn, I suppose you'd call it.'

'I'm afraid I canna help ye,' said Andy.

'This woman must have known you, sir, or she wouldn't have been carrying your name about with her . . . '

'It doesna necessarily follow,' said Andy.

'It suggests a connection, sir,' said Halliday. 'I'd be obliged if you would come along to the mortuary with me and . . . '

'I thought you said the features were

unrecognisable,' interrupted Tony.

'That's true, sir, but there might be something about the clothes or the appearance of the body that this gentleman might identify.'

'I'm quite certain I know nothing about her,' began Andy, but the Superintendent interrupted him apologetically.

'Afraid I shall have to insist, sir,' he said.

'When do you want me to come?' asked Andy.

'There's no time like now, sir. I've a car outside the pier. It won't take more than a few minutes.'

Andy shrugged his shoulders.

'Let's get it over, then,' he said resignedly.

Just as they were going, the Superintendent turned to Sharon.

'Why did you ask what colour the woman's hair was, miss?' he said.

'I — I don't know ... I just — wondered,' she answered.

'Rather a queer thing to wonder, wasn't it? Unless you had some special reason?'

'It — it just came into my mind ... '

He gave her a long and rather searching look.

'I see, miss. It just came into your mind . . . '

He nodded thoughtfully and went out with Andy.

As they came into the passage, Gilbert came out of his dressing room. He was carrying a brown paper parcel under his arm.

'Taking the washing home?' said Andy.

'Yes,' retorted Gilbert curtly. 'Any objection?'

He pushed past them without another word and went out the stage door.

Halliday frowned.

'Who was that, sir?' he asked.

'One of my company — why?' answered Andy.

'His face seemed familiar. What's his name, sir?'

'Gilbert — Howard Gilbert.'

Halliday shook his head in a puzzled way.

'Gilbert, eh? I wonder where I've seen him before?'

5

'You nearly put the cat among the pigeons, Sharon,' said Tony. 'What did you ask about her hair for?'

'Why didn't you and Andy tell him about the girl and the packet?' she said.

'Yes, why didn't you?' asked Vera. 'I think it was awfully silly not to. If the police find out there'll be a lot of trouble.'

'You heard what Andy said. It's not our affair and he doesn't want to get mixed up in it,' said Tony.

'But the girl was killed — it's murder,' protested Sharon.

'Sharon's right, Tony,' said Vera. 'We ought to have told that policeman all we know.'

'We don't really know anything,' said Tony.

'You know about that horrible fat man,' said Sharon.

'A fat man?' said Vera sharply.

'Yes — like a great slug. What's his

name — Beatal . . . ?'

Vera caught her breath with a sudden hiss and her face went white.

'What's the matter?' asked Tony.

She recovered herself quickly.

'Nothing,' she said. 'It — it was the name. I've always been scared to death of beetles. Come on, Sharon. Let's go and get changed.'

They came out into the passage to find Beryl talking to a tall, thin, elderly man with grey hair and gold pince-nez. She looked round as they came out of the dressing room.

'Oh, here's Miss Lee now,' she said. 'Vera, somebody wants to see you.'

'*Me?*' said Vera in surprise.

'Miss Lee?' said the elderly man with a smile. She nodded.

'My name is Hargreaves, Miss Lee — Wilson Hargreaves.'

Vera's face changed.

'You were expecting me, I think,' he went on, still smiling pleasantly.

'Yes, I was expecting you,' she said. 'Tony, can I use your room for a minute? Sharon wants to change in ours.'

'Of course,' said Tony.

'Thanks,' said Vera gratefully. 'Will you come in here, Mr. Hargreaves?'

She opened the door and he went in. She turned to the others.

'Don't wait for me,' she said. 'I've got some business to talk over.'

'Who was that I wonder?' said Beryl curiously when she had gone.

'Mr. Hargreaves!' said Sharon.

'I know, but what's he want with Vera?'

'Perhaps she's found a sugar daddy,' said Sharon.

'More like the family solicitor,' said Tony.

'Oh, do you think somebody's left Vera a fortune?' cried Beryl.

'I should say it was very unlikely,' remarked Tony. 'Still you never know. Hurry up and change, Sharon. I'll wait for you at the café opposite the pier. You coming with us, Beryl?'

'Where's Andy?' asked Beryl.

'He's — well, he's busy . . . '

Beryl sighed.

'Oh, well, I may as well have tea with you, then,' she said.

★ ★ ★

Inside Tony's dressing room, Vera faced the elderly man with the gold-rimmed pince-nez.

'Well?' she said.

'Beautiful weather but the nights are treacherous,' he remarked.

'You can always stay indoors after sunset,' she answered.

'Correct,' said Mr. Hargreaves briskly. 'Now, Miss Lee, I think you have something for me. A small packet.'

'I was told you would be coming,' she said.

'You have the packet?'

'Not here . . . '

'Where?'

'I thought it was safer to keep it at my lodgings.'

He nodded appreciatively.

'That was sensible,' he remarked. 'You have carried out your instructions admirably.'

'I wish I knew a little more about it,' she said.

'There is no reason why you should.

You were required to do a certain thing — you have done it. So far as you are concerned the matter is at an end, or will be when you have placed the packet in my hands.'

'I didn't bargain for murder,' she snapped.

His face hardened.

'What do you mean — murder?' he said curtly.

'A girl's body was found under the pier this afternoon,' she answered. 'She'd been strangled.'

'I know nothing about it,' he said smoothly. 'If you are wise, Miss Lee, you will know nothing about it either. Now, as soon as you are ready, we will go and complete our transaction . . . '

Anthony Wayne got back to the Dome early that evening and he was making-up when Billy burst into the dressing room.

'Hello,' he said. 'You're early.'

'The girls and I tried to find a place for tea but everywhere was jammed packed tight,' said Tony, 'so they went back to their digs and I came on here. Have you heard about all the excitement?'

'Which lot of excitement are you talking about?' asked Billy.

'Good grief! Don't tell me there's more than one,' exclaimed Tony.

'There is, you know,' said Billy. 'Not so serious as finding that poor woman's body, but jolly queer all the same. Vera's had a burglar.'

'A burglar?'

'Fact,' said Billy. 'I've just left her. She's awfully upset. Somebody went to her digs during the matinée — it's one of those places where the front door is always open, you know the kind of thing? They got into her room and turned the place upside down.'

Tony looked interested.

'Do they know who it was?' he asked.

'Some little sneak-thief, out for anything he could pick up, I suppose.'

'Was anything stolen?'

Billy shook his head.

'No. According to Vera there wasn't anything worth stealing. Nobody saw anyone. The landlady was down in the basement and the other lodgers were all out. None of the other rooms were touched, though. Queer, eh?'

'Very queer,' said Tony, frowning thoughtfully. 'Very queer, indeed.'

'We seem to have landed in a hotbed of mystery and mayhem. I say, you and Andy must have been right about that girl in the basket last night.'

'I'm afraid we were,' said Tony.

'It's a terrible thing you know,' said Billy, his usually sunny face clouded. 'She was such a pretty girl . . . '

Andy came in. He looked very white and rather shaken.

'How did you get on, Andy?' asked Tony.

'It wasna a pleasant experience,' said Andy. He sat down in a chair with a sigh of relief. 'I popped into the pub over the road for a brandy before I came in.'

'Where have you been?' asked Billy.

'With Superintendent Halliday to the mortuary,' said Andy.

'Good Lord. No wonder you wanted a brandy!' exclaimed Billy.

'Aye. I wouldna like the experience often.'

'*Was* it the girl?' said Tony.

Andy gave a little shudder.

'You couldna tell,' he said.

'What made you go? Do the police know that you found the girl in the basket?' asked Billy.

'No, I didna tell them anything about it.'

'What made them come to you, then?'

'They found a scrap of paper with my name on it in a pocket of her suit,' said Andy.

'How on earth did that get there?' demanded Billy.

Andy shook his head.

'I've no idea.'

'Why didn't you tell them about finding the girl in the basket?' asked Billy.

'Because then we'd all have been involved,' answered Andy. 'They might even suspect that one of us had something to do with it . . . '

'I'm not sure they wouldn't be right,' put in Tony.

'Somebody pinched that packet out of this room — and it wasn't Beatal . . . '

Billy stared at him.

'Stole the packet?'

'Yes. Sometime during the show last night,' said Tony.

'Anybody might have come in. The stage door's always open during the show. It couldna have been anyone in the company. Ye had the packet before we went up for the finalé and there was no opportunity afterwards.'

'Why should any of us want the thing?' demanded Billy.

'Why should anybody want it?' said Tony.

'Aye,' said Andy. 'It must be very valuable. I still think it was Beatal who took it.'

'Then why did he bother to talk to me in the café?'

'Do you think he killed the girl?' said Billy.

'He's capable of anything,' answered Tony. 'The question is — *when* could he have killed her?'

'It must have been between matinée and the evening show,' said Andy. 'There'd have been nobody here then.'

'Why should she come here at that time?' said Tony.

'To get the packet from you,' said Billy.

'But surely she wouldn't have come until later,' said Tony. 'She knew I was bringing it back with me from my digs. She must have known there'd be nobody here at that time . . .'

'Aye,' said Andy slowly. 'But she was wrong. There was somebody . . .'

'Yes.' Tony's voice was very grave. There was somebody — *waiting* . . .'

6

Just outside the town of Westpool there is a group of bungalows near the edge of the cliff that can be rented furnished for the season. The rents are high but the bungalows are comfortable and sufficiently far apart to insure privacy.

In the living room of one of these, Mr. Wilson Hargreaves was pacing up and down restlessly. He looked both annoyed and worried. Lolling in an easy chair was a dark-haired, middle-aged man, with a hard face and a cynical twist to his thin mouth. He looked the type of man who could be very unpleasant if things did not go the way he wanted them to.

'You're quite sure,' he said, not for the first time, 'that this girl isn't pulling a fast one?'

Hargreaves pulled gently at his high-bridged nose.

'Why should she?' he asked.

'Never mind why. Are you sure she

isn't?' snapped the other.

His voice was harsh and metallic.

'All I'm definitely sure about, Renton, is that the packet has disappeared,' admitted Hargreaves.

'The whole thing sounds phoney to me,' said Renton.

'Do you have to use these beastly Americanisms?' said Hargreaves irritably.

'Why not?' said Renton. 'They're expressive.'

'I find them extremely irritating,' said Hargreaves.

Renton shrugged his broad shoulders.

'Sorry,' he grunted. 'I'll anglicise it, if you like. Did someone really steal that packet from her lodgings, or is she making up a story to account for not handing it over to you?'

'There's no reason for her to do that,' said Hargreaves. 'She didn't know what was in it.'

'She only had to open it.'

'Even then she wouldn't realise its value.'

'She would if someone had put her wise.'

'There may be something in that,' agreed Hargreaves thoughtfully.

'When there's a question of something like two million pounds involved, there may be a great deal in it,' said Renton. 'What was the idea of choosing this girl, Lee, in the first place? A singer or something in a cheap little concert party . . . '

'That was the idea. Nobody would be likely to suspect her.'

'Somebody obviously did.'

'Yes, it went wrong somehow. The plan was to concentrate the attention on the other girl, Jill Manners, who was carrying a dummy packet exactly like the real one. She didn't know it was a dummy.'

'That's were it came unstuck. She got scared of something on the train and chucked the packet into the very compartment where the Lee girl was travelling with the rest of the concert party. A case of putting the cat in the aviary with a vengeance.'

'She wasn't scared for nothing,' said Hargreaves. 'Her body was pulled out of the sea this afternoon. She'd been strangled.'

Renton sat up quickly.

'What!' he exclaimed. 'Beatal's work, I suppose?'

'Or the other lot,' said Hargreaves.

'We don't know who they are . . . '

'No, I wish we did.'

Renton got up. He walked to a table containing drinks and poured himself out a stiff whisky. At one gulp he drained the glass of neat spirit.

'We've got to find that packet, Hargreaves,' he said. 'We've got to. We can't let a fortune slip through our fingers at the last lap.'

'We're not going to,' replied Hargreaves grimly. 'The question is — where is it?'

At precisely that moment, in the sitting room of his suite in one of Westpool's luxurious hotels, Simon Beatal was asking the same question. He was sitting, clad in a flowered silk dressing gown, with a big-bowled brandy glass beside him, talking to the thin-faced little man who had visited Howard Gilbert.

'The question is — where is it?' he said thoughtfully. 'A difficult problem, Chives, but not unsolvable. To an intelligent man, sir, nothing is insurmountable. Let us look at the thing logically.' He paused to take a sip of brandy. 'The packet was in the possession of Mr. Wayne up to the time they made the discovery of that unfortunate girl's body in the basket. While they were — er — engaged on the stage, I, with your invaluable assistance, sir, removed the body from the basket and substituted the dummy from the waxworks.'

'Why you took the risk of doin' that, I don't know,' interjected Chives.

'The answer is surely obvious, sir,' retorted Simon Beatal. 'Had the body remained there, these concert party people would have been forced to send for the police. I had already informed them the girl was my niece. I could not fail to have been dragged into the inquiry that followed. The substitution of the dummy made the whole thing ridiculous. Nobody would have believed their story of a dead body in face of it. A simple example of forethought, sir.' He gave one of his jerky laughs, and Chives stared at him.

'You must have got ice in yer veins,' he said.

'Merely the proper control of the emotions, sir,' said Beatal. 'To continue our reasoning. Nobody from outside came in at that period to take the packet. I was, myself, considering searching for it but I judged, correctly, that there would not be time. Therefore, either it is still in Mr. Wayne's possession, and he was lying when he told me it was not, or some other member of the concert party stole it. You agree, sir?'

'It sounds reasonable,' admitted Chives.

'The next step is to discover which of these conclusions is the right one, sir,' said Simon Beatal.

'How are you going to do that?'

The fat man took another sip of brandy.

'I am giving the matter a great deal of consideration, sir,' he answered. 'I shall shortly reach a decision.'

'And then what?' asked Chives.

'There is a time for thinking and a time for action, sir,' answered Simon Beatal. 'That will be the time for action.'

Sharon came out of her dressing room fumbling with the hook at the back of her dress. As she walked towards the steps leading up to the stage she met Andy and Tony coming down.

'It's a good house, isn't it, Andy?' she said.

'Packed like sardines,' answered Andy, rubbing his hands.

'Let me do that,' said Tony seeing her still fiddling with the back of her dress. 'Keep still.' He deftly fixed the hook. 'There you are.'

She smiled brightly at him.

'Thanks.'

'What are you doing after the show tonight?' he asked.

'Is that a prelude to an invitation,' she said.

'Yes.'

'Well? Go on — tell me the rest,' she said.

'There's a dance at the Blue Grotto. I thought perhaps you'd like to come . . . '

'I'd love to.'

72

'Well, get changed as quickly as you can after the finalé,' he said. 'If we hurry we can get away before the others.'

'I see — just *a deux*?'

'Strictly.'

'All right. I'll be ready.' She waved her hand and hurried up the steps to the stage.

He went along the passage towards his dressing room and met Andy coming back.

'Ye know about the new finalé we're trying tonight?' said Andy, adjusting the false nose he had been to get.

'Yes, don't worry,' answered Tony.

Vera came out of her room and Andy stopped her.

'Dinna forget the new finalé,' he said. 'I've told the others.'

'Right oh,' she said.

'It makes a difference to your position, you know,' he said. 'Ye'll no forget that?'

'No, all right,' she said absently.

He looked at her critically.

'Are ye feeling all right? You don't look too well . . . '

'I've got a bit of a headache, that's all,' she said.

'That business at your digs — it upset ye, maybe?'

'It did rather,' she admitted.

'It was lucky ye didna lose anything,' he said with a sudden keen glance. 'Ye might have had something there that was very valuable.'

He hurried away and she looked after him suspiciously.

There was something in the tone of his voice that made her feel uneasy . . .

* * *

The Blue Grotto was packed. It was so unpleasantly packed that after half an hour of attempting to dance on the crowded floor Tony and Sharon gave it up and came out into the moonlit coolness of the summer night.

'Phew!' said Tony, wiping his perspiring face with his handkerchief. 'I feel as if I'd had a Turkish bath.'

'It was a bit warm,' said Sharon who looked surprisingly cool.

'Stifling! I ought to have guessed it would be crowded,' he said apologetically.

'Pity. It was a first-class band, but no room to dance! All you could do was stand still and shuffle. I'm awfully sorry Sharon.'

'Don't be silly, Tony. It wasn't your fault.'

'What shall we do? Try somewhere else?'

'I don't suppose any of the other places will be any better,' she said. 'Let's go for a walk along the beach. It's a lovely night.'

'Fine,' said Tony enthusiastically. 'There's nothing I'd like better. Which way shall we go?'

'Do you think the pier will still be open?' asked Sharon. 'I'd like to pop into the Dome. I left the key of my digs on my dressing table.'

'The pier will be open,' said Tony. 'But I'm doubtful about the stage door . . . '

'We could try, couldn't we?' she said. 'My landlady goes to bed awfully early and I don't want to have to knock her up. Then we needn't hurry.'

Tony agreed and they set off along the front. Simon Beatal, who had been sitting patiently on a seat watching the entrance to the Blue Grotto, got up and walked slowly along behind them.

It was a short walk to the pier and in a few minutes they were standing outside the stage door. It was shut but when Tony tried the handle it opened easily.

'There you are,' said Sharon. 'It *is* open.'

'And somebody has left the light on in the passage,' said Tony.

They entered and the door closed behind them.

'Isn't there a watchman or a fireman or something?' said Sharon.

'Probably,' said Tony. 'That would account for the light. Hello,' he called. 'Anybody about?'

His voice echoed along the passage but there was no reply.

'I'll slip into my dressing room and get the key,' said Sharon. 'I shan't be a minute.'

She went over to the door and opened it, switching on the light.

'Tony,' she called sharply a second later. 'Come here.'

He hurried over to her.

'Look,' she said, pointing. 'Somebody has been here. The whole place has been turned upside down.'

He looked in over her shoulder. The room was a chaotic muddle. The contents of the dressing table had been swept on to the floor and dresses had been pulled from their hooks and strewn in every direction.

'I say,' exclaimed Tony, 'this is too bad, you know. I wonder if the other rooms are in the same state.'

He went to the room next door, turned the handle and looked in. Here, too, the whole place was in a muddle. He went quickly in turn to all the dressing rooms. They were all in the same state. Somebody had made a thorough search. He came back to Sharon.

'They're all in the same state,' he said indignantly. 'It's disgraceful! The whole place has been ransacked. I'm going to find someone in authority and complain.'

'Don't you dare to go and leave me here alone,' she said.

'I suppose we ought to make certain that there's nobody still about,' he said.

Sharon looked at him with frightened eyes.

'You don't really think there is, do you?' she gasped.

'There could be. I'll go and have a look round.'

She grabbed at his arm.

'You'll do nothing of the kind,' she said firmly. 'You'll stay just where you are!'

'But we must make certain there's nobody still here,' he said. 'We can't leave the place until we're sure . . . '

'Well, then, I'm coming with you,' she declared determinedly. 'I'm not going to be left alone.'

'Good evening, sir,' remarked a voice behind them. They turned swiftly to the doorway. Simon Beatal was leaning against the door frame.

'Oh, it's you again, is it?' said Tony.

'I ventured to suggest, sir, that we should meet again,' said Beatal. He came farther into the room. 'I trust this time you will introduce me to your charming companion, sir.'

'What are you doing here?' demanded Tony angrily.

'I saw you come in, sir. The opportunity presented itself for a little talk.'

'I've not the slightest wish to talk to you,' snapped Tony rudely.

'Perhaps you would prefer to call it a business conference, sir.'

'I should prefer to call it nothing.'

'Come, come, sir,' said Simon Beatal soothingly. 'You are impetuous. You are not allowing your natural perspicacity to overrule a certain unfounded antipathy to myself. I am prepared to discuss business, sir. There is a great deal of money involved in this matter. You will not find me ungenerous, sir.'

'That is the second time you've tried to bribe me,' said Tony.

'An unpleasant word, sir,' said Simon Beatal. 'Shall we say remuneration for services rendered?'

'You can call it what you like. It makes no difference.'

'You are behaving foolishly, sir.'

'That is a matter of opinion,' said Tony.

'Exactly, sir — my opinion. You are, naturally, unaware of the vast issues involved . . . '

'Why don't you tell us what it's all about?' said Sharon.

'Because it is far better that you should remain in ignorance,' he answered. 'Come, come, sir. You have got mixed up in this matter by an unfortunate accident. It is no concern of yours. Why not stop being obstinate, sir? The packet is of no value to you . . .'

'Is that what you've been searching the place for?' asked Sharon.

Simon Beatal turned towards her quickly.

'I fail to comprehend your meaning,' he said.

'Haven't you been here before tonight?' said Sharon. 'Wasn't it you who turned all the dressing rooms upside down?'

'The dressing rooms have been searched?' he demanded sharply.

'You know very well they have,' said Tony.

'You attribute knowledge to me, sir, that I do not possess,' retorted Simon Beatal.

'Well. Somebody's been here,' said Sharon. 'Just look at the place.'

The black, beady snake-like eyes in

their folds of fat turned from side to side slowly.

'I see,' said Simon Beatal. 'Somebody has been looking for the packet, sir.'

'What is so valuable about this packet?' asked Tony curiously.

Beatal laughed, his little jerky, mirthless laugh.

'Regarding that, sir, I'm afraid I cannot enlighten you,' he said.

'He told you, Mr. Wayne, it's no concern of yours,' said a fresh voice, breaking in from the doorway. With remarkable swiftness for so fat a man, Simon Beatal swung round.

'Hargreaves!' he exclaimed.

Hargreaves came into the room followed by Renton.

'Quite a surprise, eh, Mr. Beatal?' he said.

'Look here, what is this?' demanded Tony. 'A gathering of the clans?'

'I should hardly call it that, Mr. Wayne,' said Hargreaves.

'Nicely put, sir,' said Simon Beatal. 'Quite a coincidence this meeting, if I may say so.'

'There's no coincidence about it,' snapped Renton. 'We followed you.'

'Two minds with but a single thought, sir.'

'If you put any value on that fat hide of yours, you'd better keep out of this,' said Renton angrily.

'There is no point in being rude, sir,' answered Beatal, 'or indulging in empty threats.'

'They're not empty. You'll find that out quick enough, if you don't stop sticking your ugly nose in our business . . . '

'*Your* business, sir?' Simon Beatal managed in some way to make the question sound like an insult. Renton uttered an exclamation and raised a clenched fist.

'I've a good mind to . . . ' he snarled, but Hargreaves stopped him.

'That'll do, Renton,' he said curtly.

'I know you,' said Sharon suddenly to Hargreaves. 'You came to see Vera Lee this afternoon.'

Hargreaves looked disconcerted and Beatal was quick to notice it.

'Who is Vera Lee?' he asked quickly.

'One of our company,' answered Sharon.

'This is interesting, sir, very interesting.' Simon Beatal raised his eyebrows. 'May I be permitted to inquire why you came to see this lady?'

'You may,' said Hargreaves.

'But you won't get an answer,' sneered Renton.

'I'm rather curious myself — now,' remarked Tony.

'I wouldn't get too curious,' snapped Renton.

'If I might hazard a guess, sir,' said Simon Beatal, 'it was connected with a certain packet?'

'Vera couldn't have had anything to do with that,' said Sharon.

'She couldn't have taken it out of my dressing room,' said Tony. 'She had no opportunity.'

Hargreaves laughed shortly.

'You find something in the situation amusing, sir?' asked Simon Beatal.

Renton made an impatient gesture.

'Cut out all the smarmy talk, Beatal,' he cried. 'You've got the packet and we want it. Come on — hand it over.'

'You are mistaken, sir,' began Beatal.

'Hand it over!' snapped Renton. His hand came out of his pocket and there was a glint as the light fell on a small automatic pistol. Sharon gave a little cry and shrank back against Tony.

'Put that away!' ordered Hargreaves sternly.

'I'm sick of all this fooling around,' snarled Renton.

'Put that away, I tell you,' said Hargreaves. Renton hesitated and then he reluctantly put the little weapon back in his pocket.

'You want to handle everything with kid gloves,' he said disgustedly.

'I dislike violence,' said Hargreaves. 'Mr. Beatal will, I am sure, agree with me that it is unnecessary.'

'Will he?' sneered Renton. 'What about the girl?'

'I don't know what you mean, sir,' said Beatal.

'I mean the girl you strangled and flung in the sea,' said Renton brutally.

Sharon gave a little cry and moved closer to Tony.

'Oh,' she breathed, staring at the fat man in terror, 'it wasn't *you* . . . '

'It's no concern of ours,' interrupted Hargreaves. 'If Mr. Beatal was so unwise as to lose his self-control in that direction, there is no reason why we should follow such a bad example.'

'You are wrong, sir,' said Simon Beatal. 'I am in no way responsible. I deplore violence . . . '

'I'm all for it — at the right time,' said Renton.

'All we are interested in, Beatal,' said Hargreaves, 'is your unauthorised visit to Miss Lee's lodgings.'

'You are wrong again, sir. You appear to be completely misinformed about these matters.'

'You're lying,' grated Renton. 'You've got that packet . . . '

'You should use your intelligence, sir, if you possess such a commodity,' said Simon Beatal. 'If I were in possession of the packet should I be here now? An irrefutable argument, sir.'

'There's something in that,' muttered Hargreaves.

'He's bluffing,' snarled Renton. 'Let me have a go at him. I'll soon make him tell the truth.'

'No,' snapped Hargreaves.

'What's the good of being squeamish? This isn't a kids' bun-fight.'

'We'll handle it my way,' said Hargreaves coldly.

'You make me sick!' said Renton, his face white with suppressed fury.

'I congratulate you, sir. Your attitude to the situation is one of admirable restraint,' said Simon Beatal. 'These strong-arm methods, advocated by your associate, would be of no avail. I do not possess the packet — unfortunately.'

'Then who has?' demanded Renton.

'That, sir, is what I am endeavouring to discover . . . '

At that moment the light in the dressing room and the passage outside went out.

Sharon uttered a startled cry. Renton muttered an oath. There was a faint sound — the sound of scurrying footsteps along the passage.

'Who's there?' cried Hargreaves. 'There's

somebody in the building besides us . . . '

Tony and Sharon pushed their way out into the passage. They saw the stage door open and, in the light that streamed in from the pier, caught a glimpse of a figure as it slipped out.

It was the figure of a woman.

The stage door shut with a thud that echoed in the darkness of the passage.

'Tony,' said Sharon huskily and he felt her trembling against him. 'Did you see who it was?'

'No,' he answered.

'It was the girl — the girl who was killed,' said Sharon shakily. 'I saw her face — for a moment — in the light . . . '

'But that's impossible.'

'It was I tell you, it was . . . ' She suddenly buried her face on his shoulder and began to cry . . .

7

Hargeave's voice came sharply out of the darkness:

'Did you say it was the girl who was killed?' he asked.

'Yes, yes — it was.' Sharon's voice was muffled against Tony's shoulder.

'Are you suggesting it was a ghost?' asked Simon Beatal.

'Scared, Beatal?' sneered Renton.

'There is no valid reason why I should be, sir.'

'You're sure it was the same girl, Sharon?' asked Tony.

She raised her head.

'Yes . . . I saw her face clearly . . . '

'Jill Manners,' muttered Hargreaves.

'Is that her name?' asked Tony quickly.

'I — I don't understand,' said Sharon. She was still trembling and her voice was husky. 'She's dead . . . They found her body . . . '

'An obvious error,' remarked Simon Beatal.

'You should know,' said Tony.

'If you are insinuating, sir — 'began the fat man.

'She's your niece, isn't she?' interrupted Tony sarcastically.

Hargreaves laughed.

'Is that what he told you?' he asked.

'A necessary adjustment of the facts, sir,' said Simon Beatal.

Renton had gone along to the stage door and opened it. He looked out.

'There's a hook on the door,' said Tony. 'Keep it open.'

Renton found the hook and slipped it into a ring in the wall. The light from outside streamed through into the passage and dispelled the darkness.

'Let's go, Tony,' whispered Sharon. 'Let's get out of this place . . . '

The figure of a man suddenly appeared in the open doorway.

'What's all this?' it demanded in a surly voice. 'What's going on here?' He came farther into the passage and they saw that he was the pier attendant. 'You've no right in 'ere, yer know . . . '

'Are you responsible for locking this place up?' demanded Tony.

'Never you mind what I'm responsible for,' said the attendant. 'You just clear out of 'ere — quick, see?'

'Excellent advice, sir,' said Simon Beatal. 'There seems no point in our prolonging our little conference.'

'I ought ter report this to the piermaster,' said the attendant.

'I'm going to do a little reporting, myself,' snapped Tony. 'This place was left open and somebody has been in and ransacked our dressing rooms . . . '

'So *that's* what she was doing,' said Hargreaves.

'Do you belong to the concert party?' asked the attendant.

'Yes. We came back because this lady had left her key and we found the stage door open,' said Tony.

'A man's entitled to 'is supper, ain't 'e?' The attendant sounded slightly aggrieved. 'I've never 'ad no trouble before.' He felt for the passage light switch. ''Allo, what's the matter with the lights?'

90

'I don't know,' said Tony. 'They all went out.'

'Fuse gone, I expect,' said the attendant. He took a torch from the pocket of his uniform. 'I'll 'ave a look at the switchboard.'

'Let's go, Tony,' said Sharon.

'That's right, miss,' said the attendant. 'If yer all go, I can lock up. I like to see me wife now an' again — even if it's only just ter say good night.'

'A laudable ambition, sir,' said Simon Beatal. 'I will be the first to set a good example. Good night, sir. Good night, gentlemen.'

'We're coming with you,' said Renton grimly.

'We do not go in the same direction, sir.'

'I think we do, Beatal — I think we do,' remarked Hargreaves.

Beatal uttered one of his little jerky laughs.

'As you wish, sir,' he said. 'I'm gratified to think that you should find so much pleasure in my company.'

He went out with Hargreaves and Renton

on either side of him, still laughing his unpleasant little mirthless laugh.

The attendant came back.

'Somebody pulled down the main switch,' he said. 'Funny goings on, if yer ask me . . .'

They left him, muttering and grumbling. When they were out in the moonlit summer night, Sharon looked up at Tony.

'Tony,' she said with a troubled face. 'That *was* the girl — the red-haired girl who was on the train.'

'You're quite *sure* of that, Sharon?' he asked.

She nodded emphatically.

'Yes,' she answered without hesitation. 'Quite sure.'

He frowned in a puzzled way.

'Then who,' he said, 'was the other one? The one they took out of the sea . . .'

★ ★ ★

'Vera!' Vera Lee turned quickly as Tony called to her from the door of his dressing room.

'Yes?'

'I want to talk to you,' he said. 'Will you come and have tea somewhere after the matinée?'

'I've got a headache . . . '

'A cup of tea will do it good,' he persisted.

She frowned.

'I don't think I can,' she said. 'I'm going home to lie down.'

'It's rather important — it's about Hargreaves.'

A startled look came into her face.

'What do you know about Hargreaves?' she asked sharply.

'Let's discuss it at tea, shall we?' he answered.

'All right,' she said at last.

★ ★ ★

Superintendent Halliday was sitting in his office at the police station. It was a small room which was almost completely filled by the big desk at which he sat and a couple of filing cabinets.

Halliday was gently chewing at the end of a pencil and frowning. The door opened and Detective-Sergeant Soames came in. He was a thin, rather melancholy-looking man.

'Well?' asked Halliday, 'did you get anything?'

Soames shook his head.

'Nothing, sir,' he answered gloomily. 'We've tried all the hotels.'

'Boarding houses?'

'Quite a lot of them too. Collins and Vance are still working on the rest. Up to now there's no woman reported missing.'

'Maybe she wasn't staying in Westpool,' Halliday sighed. 'That's going to make it more difficult. We can't get much farther until we can identify her.'

'I'm pretty sure that man, McKay, knows something, sir.'

'And that girl, what's-her-name, Roy — Sharon Roy. She must have had a reason for asking about the colour of the hair. There's something fishy there. Why should the dead woman have been carrying McKay's name in her pocket if she didn't know him? Did you ask London to check up on him?'

'Yes sir.'

'That may give us a line. If she was strangled in the Dome Pavilion it would have been easy to dump her body over the pier, eh?'

'There's something in that, sir,' agreed Soames.

'There's a man calling himself Howard Gilbert in that concert party,' Halliday went on. 'Big chap, singer or something. I've seen him before somewhere. It was nothing to do with the stage — something unpleasant. Find out all you can about him, too.'

'Do you think he's in it, sir?'

Halliday made an impatient gesture.

'I don't know who's in it. I don't even know what 'it' is. All I know at present is that an unknown woman has been murdered and that some of these concert-party people may know something about it. Only *may*. We don't know that they do.'

'Maybe we'll know more when we hear from London, sir.'

'What we want, Soames, is the woman's identity,' said Halliday. 'Once we know who she was, we'll probably know why she was killed and that should give us a direct line to the killer.'

'In the meanwhile, sir, I'll find out all I can about this man, Gilbert.'

'Yes, do that. Howard Gilbert?' The Superintendent rubbed his forehead. 'I'm quite sure that that wasn't his name when I met him before.'

★   ★   ★

Tony and Vera sat at the only available table in a small café off the front. All the rest were full and they had been lucky to secure this table. Already there was a queue outside the place.

A waitress who appeared to be suffering with a permanent cold in the head approached their table.

'Wotcher want?' she demanded with a sniff.

'We'd like some tea, please,' said Tony pleasantly.

'The set tea's three and six,' said the waitress and sniffed again.

'I only want tea, nothing to eat,' said Vera. She looked a little pale and weary.

'Just a pot of tea for two,' said Tony.

The waitress sniffed.

'We only do the set tea,' she said.

'All right, we'll have the set tea whatever-it-is,' agreed Tony.

'Salad, bread and butter, scones and jam,' said the waitress. 'Cakes is extra.'

'That's a full meal,' said Tony.

'You wait till you see it,' said the waitress disparagingly and sniffed twice. 'The salad's only two leaves of lettuce, a round of cucumber, an' 'alf a tomato. The rest of it yer could swaller in two mouthfuls.'

'I wonder people don't complain,' said Tony.

'Complain?' echoed the waitress scornfully. 'What's the use o' complainin'? It's either that or nothin'.'

She departed with a louder sniff than usual.

'It's funny what people will put up with when they're on holiday,' remarked Tony.

'You wanted to talk about Hargreaves,' said Vera curtly. 'What about him?'

'Who is he?' asked Tony.

'I don't know,' answered Vera.

He looked at her in surprise.

'You don't know . . . ' he began and she interrupted him.

'It sounds absurd, doesn't it?' she said. 'But it's the truth. I never saw him before — yesterday afternoon,'

'What did he come for? Look here, Vera,' he added as she frowned. 'I don't want to pry into your private affairs but there's something pretty queer going on and it may lead to trouble . . . '

'I know. I wish I'd had nothing to do with it.'

'With what? Hargreaves and the packet?'

'How did you know about that?' she asked quickly,

'Never mind now,' he answered. 'I'll tell you presently. How did you get mixed up in it?'

'It was the day we left London — or rather the day before. We finished rehearsal in the morning and after a sandwich and a cup of coffee at a snack bar, I went home to pack . . . '

''Ere yer are,' broke in the waitress with a smile, banging a tray in front of them. 'They give yer a jug of 'ot water but I wouldn't use it, if I was you.'

'Why not?' asked Tony.

'You'll see when you pour the tea,' said the waitress.

'Are you as candid as this to all the customers?' he inquired, laughing.

'Why not?' She gave a prodigious sniff. 'I'm leavin' termorrer!'

She picked up the now empty tray and went away.

'That girl was right,' said Vera, pouring out the tea. 'I think they must have just added hot water to an old pot.'

'It'll be wet and warm,' said Tony.

'I'm afraid it's not even very warm,' she said.

'Tell me some more about Hargreaves,' said Tony, as he took the cup she handed to him. 'You went home after rehearsal to pack. What happened then?'

'I'd just reached the front door,' she said, 'and I was getting the key out of my bag when somebody called my name. There was a man on the other side of the road and he started to cross over towards me.'

'Did you know him?'

She shook her head.

'No, he was a stranger. I was a little bit startled but he was very polite. He apologised for bothering me and said that he understood I was going to Westpool.'

'How did he know?' asked Tony. 'Did he tell you?'

Again she shook her head.

'No. He must have found out somehow. Anyway he asked me if I'd like to earn ten pounds . . . '

'Just like that?'

'Just like that. He went to great lengths to assure me that it was all above board and quite simple. All he wanted me to do was to deliver a small packet to a friend of his. It was very valuable, he said, and he didn't want to trust it to the post.'

'What on earth made him pick on you?' asked Tony.

'That's exactly what I wanted to know,' she answered. 'He was quite frank about it. He admitted that there were certain people who were interested in the contents of the packet. He felt that they might suspect any ordinary messenger. But as I had a legitimate reason for coming to Westpool there was a good chance that they'd never catch on to me. It seemed quite plausible at the time. I was to deliver the packet to a Mr. Wilson Hargreaves who was going to call for it at the Dome.'

'And that's all?'

She nodded.

'That's all. I suppose I was silly to agree but I'd been out of work for a long time and — well, ten pounds is ten pounds when you're practically broke and it seemed a very simple thing to do.'

'You must have thought it rather queer,' said Tony.

'I did,' she answered candidly, 'but I needed that money. It was a godsend.'

He took a sip of lukewarm tea.

'What was this man like? Would you recognise him?' he asked.

'Yes, I think so — I'm sure I would. He was very polite but there was something frightening about him — really frightening.'

'Do you mean his appearance?'

'Partly. He was thin with a little dark moustache and a scar running down the side of his face. He wore large dark glasses so you couldn't see the expression of his eyes. It was almost as though he was wearing a mask.' She gave a little shiver. 'But it was his voice that was really horrible . . . '

'His voice?'

'Yes. It was steely and cold and quite emotionless. The kind of voice you'd expect a snake to have if it could talk. He reminded me of a snake.'

Tony gave her a cigarette and took one himself.

'Sounds an attractive customer,' he commented. 'So you brought the packet down with you to Westpool and Hargreaves called for it?'

'Yes. So that I would know he was the right person, he was to say: 'Beautiful weather but the nights are treacherous' and I was to reply: 'You can always stay indoors after sunset'. It was all right up to there. But when I went to get the packet for him at my digs, it had gone.'

'I wonder,' said Tony thoughtfully, 'if the same person took it who took mine — the one that was thrown into our compartment on the train?'

'That gave me a shock,' said Vera. 'I couldn't understand it. I'd got an identical packet in my suitcase . . . '

'It's pretty obvious there are two packets,' said Tony. 'It's a mix-up. Somebody's got both of 'em — and it isn't Hargreaves or Beatal . . . '

'I was warned about him — a big, fat man . . . '

'Who warned you? The man who gave you the packet?'

She nodded.

'He said he might try and pass himself off as Hargreaves. That's why he arranged the password.'

Tony wrinkled his forehead.

'Why are these people all fighting to get hold of this thing?' he muttered almost to himself. 'Two little packets. What the dickens is so valuable about them. Did Jill Manners know?'

'Jill Manners?' Vera looked at him questioningly.

'That girl on the train,' he answered. 'I wish I could get hold of her . . . '

'But she's dead.'

'She was very much alive last night,' declared Tony.

'Did you see her?' Vera leaned forward curiously.

'Sharon did,' he answered. 'She was in the Dome — searching our dressing rooms . . .'

'For the packet?' asked Vera quickly.

'I suppose so. Her packet — the one she thought I'd got. Hargreaves, Beatal and a man called Renton were there too. They each thought the other had got the packet. But somebody else has got 'em — somebody we don't as yet know anything about.'

8

Three people sat in Simon Beatal's private sitting room at the Majestic Hotel on the front at Westpool. The waiter had just brought in a tray of drinks and when he had set it down and gone, the fat man picked up a glass of brandy.

'Let us drink to our new alliance, gentlemen,' he said.

Hargreaves and Renton raised their glasses. They drank.

'And no double-crossing,' grunted Renton warningly.

'Naturally, sir, naturally,' said Simon Beatal. 'That need not be considered among gentlemen. Here's to a fair bargain, sir, and profits for all of us.'

He took a sip of brandy and smacked his lips appreciatively.

'Don't go too fast,' said Hargreaves. 'We've got to get that packet before there's any question of profits.'

'I am aware of that, sir,' said the fat

man. 'It should not be beyond the capacity of our combined intelligence.'

'You make it sound like a walkover,' said Renton.

'No, sir. Nothing worth having can be acquired without effort.'

'Nor by drivelling platitudes,' snapped Renton irritably.

'We want to know who walked into that girl's lodgings and stole the packet,' said Hargreaves. 'The rest is easy.'

'Is it, sir?' said Beatal. He laughed. 'I wonder.'

Hargreaves gave him a sharp glance.

'What are you getting at now?' he demanded.

'Should we be any nearer our goal, sir?'

'Of course we should. If we knew who'd taken the packet . . .'

'We could get it,' finished Renton. 'You're talking nonsense, Beatal.'

'I never talk nonsense, sir. You have informed me that the packet carried by Jill Manners was a dummy, designed to hoodwink any person who, like myself, was interested. I confess I was completely taken in . . .'

'Come to the point,' interrupted Renton rudely.

'The point, sir, is this. Are you quite sure that the packet entrusted to Miss Lee was not in the same category, sir?'

'That's ridiculous . . . ' said Hargreaves.

'Indeed, sir?'

'The whole idea was to focus attention on Jill Manners while the Lee girl remained completely unsuspected . . . '

'You are too trusting, sir.' Simon Beatal laughed. 'A bad fault, if I may say so. These elaborate precautions taken by your associate . . . A little too elaborate, sir.' He laughed again.

'Cut out the trimmings and speak plainly,' broke in Renton.

'I will, sir. If your associate, Mr. Granger, wished to — double-cross, was the expression you used, sir, I believe? If Mr. Granger wished to double-cross you, these arrangements would provide him with a wonderful opportunity, sir.'

Hargreaves uttered a sudden exclamation.

'Are you suggesting that Granger kept the real packet?' he exclaimed.

'I suggest it as a possibility, sir,' answered Simon Beatal. 'He had already double-crossed Jill Manners. Is there any reason why he should not have extended the plan to embrace yourselves? Ostensibly Miss Lee is to deliver the packet to you. Very unfortunately — but extremely opportunely — the packet is stolen before it can reach your hands.'

'You mean it was *Granger* who stole it?' said Hargreaves.

'Come, come, sir,' said Simon Beatal impatiently. 'Do I have to explain in words of one syllable? He can swear that the packet was given to Miss Lee . . . '

Renton uttered an oath.

'If I thought the swine had done that I'd . . . '

'Be quiet,' snapped Hargreaves. 'We've no proof that Beatal's right. Granger was in London — I know that for a fact — I was talking to him on the phone just before I went to the Dome to see the Lee girl . . . '

'He rang you up, sir?' Simon Beatal laughed. 'Naturally. He would not have attended to the matter himself, of course.

108

His object would be to appear entirely innocent. An alibi, sir.'

'But,' objected Hargreaves, 'he wouldn't have known that she'd leave the packet in her lodgings . . . '

'His emissary could, sir. You may depend upon it that if she hadn't left it in her lodgings another way would have been found . . . '

'I'm going straight up to London,' snarled Renton. 'If there's any truth in the idea of yours . . . '

'Don't be too impetuous, sir,' remonstrated Beatal. 'Would it not be, shall I say, more diplomatic, to get Mr. Granger to come to Westpool?'

He looked from one to the other and there was a world of meaning in his small black, beady eyes.

'Yes,' said Hargreaves softly. 'Yes, I think perhaps it would.'

Simon Beatal laughed.

★   ★   ★

Beryl Cameron came in the stage door that evening early. Her usually pleasant face wore a worried frown. As she came level with Andy's dressing room he came out quickly.

'Andy . . . ' she began but he interrupted her.

'I canna stop now,' he said hastily, 'I'm just going through to the box office.'

He moved away but she went after him.

'Surely it can wait for a minute,' she said, 'I want to talk to you.'

'About the show?'

'Can't you think of anything except the show? There are other things in life . . . '

'Not in mine,' he declared.

'But there could be. Oh, Andy, don't you feel that you're missing something?'

'Aye,' he replied. 'That's why I'm going round to the box office. They were three and sixpence short on the matinée return.'

'I wasn't thinking about money . . . '

'But ye should. It's the stuff that pays your wages.'

'You're not getting any younger, Andy. Haven't you ever thought of settling down?'

'I'm always too busy settling up . . . '

She laid her hand on his arm.

'Wouldn't you like a nice cosy little flat somewhere? With someone to look after you. Doesn't it sound attractive?'

'Aye,' he replied, 'but who's going to pay the rent?'

'I've always thought that marriage should be on a fifty-fifty basis,' she said.

'Expenses are so high that ye canna get out under sixty-forty,' said Andy. 'That's what I'm getting here and the beggars are trying to do me out of three and sixpence!'

He hurried away. There were tears in Beryl's eyes as she, stared after him. Sharon came in quickly and found her still standing there looking rather disconsolate.

'What's the matter, Beryl?' she asked.

'I've just practically proposed to Andy,' answered Beryl tearfully, 'and all he can say is that he's three and sixpence short on the matinée return.'

'Men,' said Sharon disgustedly. 'They all ought to be tied in a bunch and drowned from the end of the pier!'

'Sharon,' Tony came out of his dressing

room. 'I say, I want to talk to you . . . '

She eyed him coldly.

'I'm afraid I've got to change,' she said and turned away.

He stared at her.

'I — I,' he stammered slightly. 'What's the matter?'

'There's nothing the matter,' she replied. 'But I object to people who break appointments.'

'Oh, my lord!' He suddenly remembered that he had arranged to meet her for tea this afternoon. 'I say, I'm awfully sorry . . . '

'There's no need to apologise,' she said. 'If you prefer to take Vera out to tea instead of me, I don't mind. I do object to waiting about, that's all.'

'I only took her to tea because I wanted to find out about Hargreaves,' he explained.

'You don't have to make excuses,' she said icily and went into her dressing room, shutting the door almost in his face. He went back to his own room and began slowly to change.

Andy came in after a few minutes and

found him sitting rather dejectedly staring at the floor.

'What's the matter with you?' he asked. 'Ye look as if ye'd had something that's disagreed with ye.'

'I have,' retorted Tony. 'Tea!'

Andy looked at him keenly.

'Tea?' he repeated.

Tony explained.

'Oh, weel,' said Andy unsympathetically. 'Ye ought to be thankful. At least she doesna chase ye all over the town.'

* * *

Hargreaves came quickly into the sitting room of Simon Beatal's suite at the Majestic Hotel.

'I've fixed it,' he said. 'Granger's coming.'

'Very nice work, sir.' The fat man nodded approvingly. 'What time do you anticipate he will arrive?'

'Somewhere about midnight, I should think,' said Hargreaves. 'He's coming to my bungalow.'

'That was wise, sir. Comfortable as it is

113

in this hotel there is a certain lack of privacy. I feel certain that at your house, we shall find it easier to persuade Mr. Granger to tell us the truth.'

'I'll persuade him all right,' said Renton. 'Leave that to me.'

'Did he seem at all reluctant to visit us, sir?' asked Beatal.

'Not when he heard the packet had been stolen,' answered Hargreaves. 'He was quite eager. He assured me that he would be leaving London almost at once.'

'He is coming by car, sir?'

Hargreaves nodded.

'I hope he has a pleasant journey, sir.' Simon Beatal laughed. 'I sincerely hope he has a pleasant journey . . .'

* * *

'Do you know, Andy,' said Tony wearily. 'I've never been so glad for a show to finish as I have tonight. I feel dog tired.'

'That's what comes of trying to be a detective,' said Andy, tying his tie. 'Ye're worrying yourself over this packet business.'

'You must admit it's interesting,' said Tony. He had finished changing and was all ready to go home.

'I canna make head nor tail of it,' declared Andy. 'Vera had a packet and that girl on the train — what did ye say her name was?'

'Jill Manners.'

'She had another packet,' continued Andy. 'Then there's these three men who are after the packet. Which one are they after? Who's the poor woman who was murdered? It's like trying to do a crossword puzzle on the morning after Hogmanay.'

'We seem to have got mixed up with a pretty nasty business,' said Tony.

'Aye — and I'll tell ye something,' said Andy. 'It appears to me that there's somebody in this company who knows all about it.'

'What makes you think that?' asked Tony quickly.

'Ye canna tell me that the fact that Vera was chosen to act as messenger for this unknown man, and the fact that the other girl, Jill Manners chose our compartment to get rid of *her* packet was just a coincidence,' explained Andy reasonably. 'There must have been a definite design behind it. Do you see what I mean?'

'Yes, but what was the design?' said Tony.

'I'm no wiser than you,' said Andy, shaking his head. 'Ye think that story Vera told ye was the truth?'

'Don't you?' asked Tony.

Andy shrugged his shoulders.

'I was thinking, maybe, that she knew just a wee bit more than she said. Ah, weel, I'm for me supper an' me bed.'

He slipped on his jacket and went over to the door.

'I may as well do the same,' said Tony with a sigh. He had tried to get a word with Sharon all the evening but she would have nothing to do with him. 'I suppose all the others have gone?'

'Aye, I should think we were the last,' agreed Andy.

But they were not the last. As they came out into the passage Howard Gilbert came out of his dressing room. He looked searchingly at them.

'Good night,' he said curtly. He strode quickly to the stage door and went out.

Tony looked after him, frowning.

'There's something queer about that chap,' he said. 'If there is somebody in this company who knows all about this business, I'll lay odds it's Gilbert.'

9

The clock on the mantelpiece chimed midnight.

'He should be here by now,' said Hargreaves.

'It's quite a journey,' said Renton. He walked over to the side table and poured himself a drink.

'I am looking forward to meeting your associate, Mr. Granger,' remarked Simon Beatal. 'I have a feeling that it will prove beneficial to our joint project, sir.'

'I hope you're right,' grunted Renton.

'It's only your idea, Beatal,' said Hargreaves, 'that there's been any jiggery-pokery by Granger. The packet he gave to Vera Lee may have been the genuine one.'

'When we are sure of that, sir, we can direct our energies to discovering who took it from Miss Lee's lodgings,' replied Simon Beatal. 'If my suggestion should turn out to be correct we should only be wasting our time chasing something that is completely valueless.'

'I see your point,' said Hargreaves, nodding.

'Naturally, sir. I trust that you gave him no hint that you suspected anything?'

Hargreaves shook his head.

'I only told him that the packet had been stolen,' he said. 'He sounded very upset and agitated over the telephone.'

'That would obviously have to be his reaction, sir,' said Simon Beatal.

'He'll be more agitated when he finds we've got you to share with now,' said Renton. He poured himself out another drink.

'It should make no difference to the total amount we share between us, sir.'

'How do you make that out? You've got to have an extra share,' said Renton.

'A share, sir — but not an extra one,' said Simon Beatal. 'Once the packet is in our possession, sir, there is no need why Mr. Granger should participate. A small honorarium, perhaps? He can do nothing about it, sir.' He laughed jerkily. 'The contents of the packet are no more legitimately his than — if I may say so — they are ours. You understand me, sir?'

Hargreaves looked across at Renton.

'Yes, I understand you,' he said slowly.

'I am a business man, sir,' remarked Simon Beatal. He laughed again. 'I believe in getting full value, sir — for other people's money.'

'Listen,' said Renton suddenly.

In the silence that followed they all heard the faint sound of an approaching car.

'Granger,' muttered Hargreaves.

The sound of the car grew louder. It came nearer the house and stopped. There was a long pause and then there came a ring at the bell.

Hargreaves left the room quickly. They heard him open the front door and the murmur of voices. Presently he returned accompanied by the man whom Vera had described to Anthony Wayne.

'What's all this about somebody stealing the packet?' he demanded without preliminary. And then he saw Simon Beatal. 'What's he doing here?'

'You are surprised, sir?' said the fat man. 'A natural emotion in the circumstances.'

Granger shot a suspicious glance at Hargreaves.

'What's the idea, Hargreaves?' he asked.

'Allow me to explain, sir,' said Simon Beatal. 'We have joined forces . . . '

'You have, have you?' Granger's voice was cold and cutting. 'Supposing I don't agree, what then?'

'Well,' interrupted Renton. '*What* then, eh?'

'You'll see,' snapped Granger. 'I'm not standing for anybody else in on this . . . '

'It doesn't entirely rest with you,' said Hargreaves smoothly.

'What do you mean?' retorted Granger angrily. 'The whole thing originated with me, didn't it?'

'If you will forgive the correction, sir,' put in Simon Beatal, 'it originated with David Manners.'

Granger swung round on him and his face darkened.

'You keep out of this,' he snarled. 'I was forced to take Hargreaves and Renton in, but I don't intend to have any dealings with you.'

'Cut out all that,' broke in Renton. 'Let's get down to brass tacks. Where's the packet?'

'That's what I'd like to know,' said

Granger. 'You tell me it was stolen from that girl's lodgings?'

Hargreaves nodded.

'Who stole it?' demanded Granger.

'That's what we want to know,' said Renton.

'Well, you don't have to look very far,' retorted Granger. He jerked his head in the direction of Simon Beatal.

'You are in error, sir,' said the fat man suavely. 'Should I have been so stupid as to join forces with Mr. Hargreaves and Mr. Renton if I already possessed the packet?'

'There's something very funny going on,' grunted Granger.

'That's what we think, Granger,' said Hargreaves. 'Was that the real packet you sent down by the Lee girl, or was it another dummy — like the one you gave to Jill Manners?'

'What the devil are you driving at?' Granger glared at him.

'The supposition is, sir,' said Simon Beatal, 'that the real packet is still in your possession.'

'That's a damned lie . . . '

'It works out very well for you, doesn't it?' said Renton unpleasantly. 'Two dummies to mislead everybody and you keep the real one.'

'If I'd wanted to I could have kept it in the first place,' retorted Granger.

'Granted, sir,' said Beatal. 'But you may have thought that this way would absolve you from any suspicion that you might be trying to — er — swindle your associates.' He laughed.

'That cuts both ways, doesn't it?' said Granger. 'How do *I* know that you're not trying to swindle me?'

'That's nonsense,' began Hargreaves impatiently but Granger cut him short.

'It's nothing of the sort,' he snapped harshly. 'Why shouldn't you have faked up this story that the packet was stolen from the girl's lodgings? Why should I believe that, any more than you believe me? One of you could have stolen it.'

He turned his hard eyes on Simon Beatal.

'Should we have taken the trouble to bring you all the way down here, if that was the case?' said Hargreaves.

'Yes — for the same reason you attributed to me,' retorted Granger. 'You all seem to have forgotten that somebody else knows about this business. Somebody who got wind of it in Canada after the plane crash.'

'That I agree, sir, should be taken into consideration,' said the fat man.

'Then stop flinging your damned accusations at me,' said Granger. 'You've no right in this at all. You gate-crashed your way in and . . . '

'Put a sock in it,' broke in Renton rudely. 'This isn't getting us anywhere. You say that the packet you gave this woman Lee, to bring down here, was the genuine one?'

'Of course it was . . . '

'Well, then we've got to find it.'

'That's easier said than done,' said Hargreaves. 'We've no more idea than the man in the moon who took it from the girl's rooms.'

'If none of us are doing a double-cross, it must be this other person,' said Granger.

'We don't know who he is,' grunted Renton.

'I suggest, sir, that we are not quite as ignorant of the person's identity as you make out,' interposed Simon Beatal.

'Why — do you know who it is?' demanded Hargreaves.

Simon Beatal shook his head.

'I do not, sir,' he replied. 'But I can suggest where you should look . . . '

'Where?' demanded Granger.

'Among the members of the concert party, sir. The Crimson Ramblers,' answered Simon Beatal.

* * *

At a table under a gaily striped awning on the front on the following morning, Billy, Sharon and Vera were having coffee. The sea, a shimmering blue in the hot sunshine, stretched away to a misty horizon and they could hear the sound of the lazy breakers as they broke on the beach.

'Pity we've a matinée,' said Billy. 'I'd like to spend the whole day dozing on the beach.'

'With one eye on the bathing beauties, I suppose?' said Vera.

'Of course, though I must say I haven't seen anything very special up to now.'

'Don't give up hope, Billy,' said Sharon.

'I never give up hope, darling,' grinned Billy.

'You're telling us,' said Vera.

'So far I'm very disappointed with Westpool,' said Billy, shaking his head. 'The girls with nice legs have got faces that would scare a seasoned commando and the ones with pretty faces are either knock-kneed or bandy!'

'You can't have everything,' said Sharon, laughing.

'Don't you believe it,' declared Billy with a twinkle in his eye. 'I remember when I was in Hastings . . . '

'We are not interested in your murky past,' said Vera hastily.

'There was nothing murky about her,' said Billy. 'What a smasher! Red hair — everything perfect. All the curves in the right places.'

He kissed the tips of his fingers.

'Did she fall for you?' asked Sharon.

'Fall,' echoed Billy. 'She power-dived! With all her jets at full pressure!'

'How delightful!' said Vera icily.

Billy shot her a mischievous look.

'It might have been,' he continued sadly. 'Only her husband was an all-in-wrestler at the fun fair.' He sighed. 'Loves young dream got a bit battered and bruised. I thought about her all the time I was in hospital!'

'I don't,' said Sharon, 'believe a word of it.'

'I thought I was telling it rather well,' said Billy.

'Billy, you're a beast,' said Vera.

'That's what the night nurse called me,' remarked Billy.

'You're incorrigible!' she said angrily.

The smile left his face. It became suddenly serious and there was something suspiciously like tears in his eyes.

'My brother used to call me that,' he said huskily.

'I didn't know you had a brother,' said Vera.

'I haven't — now,' he answered. 'He's dead. Poor old Jim. I was a bit of a handful to him . . . ' He got up abruptly. 'Think I'll go and have a swim. See you later.'

He walked quickly away and they looked after him as he crossed the road and disappeared down the steps to the beach.

'That's the first time I've ever seen Billy really serious,' said Sharon. 'He was — rather upset, wasn't he?'

Vera nodded. Her usually hard expression was softer.

'He must have been very fond of his brother,' she said.

Sharon nodded.

'Funny he's never mentioned him before,' she said.

* * *

'You're taking a risk, you know, coming here,' said Howard Gilbert, frowning into the mirror over his dressing table.

'I thought you'd want to know about Granger comin' down at once,' said Chives. 'Couldn't meet you this mornin'. I was with Beatal.'

'If Beatal suspects that you're working for me . . .'

'Don't worry — I'm careful,' said

Chives. 'What do you think of Beatal joinin' up with the other lot, eh?'

'It makes it easier for us,' said Gilbert.

'They're fools. They don't know Beatal,' said the little man. ''E'll use 'em until 'e gets what he wants an' then 'e'll dish the lot.'

'It might be the other way round . . .'

'Not on your life.' Chives shook his head.

'Beatal's just a great lump of cold-blooded cunning. 'E's got no conscience an' no feelin's. I've met a few tough ones in my time, but 'e beats 'em all.' He watched Gilbert select a stick of grease-paint and start to make up his face.

'I can't get used to you singin' in a bloomin' concert party,' he remarked.

Howard Gilbert smiled at his own reflection in the mirror. 'I can't get used to it myself,' he said.

10

The red-haired girl in the black suit walked quickly down the side of the Dome Pavilion, came to the stage door and hesitated for a moment before turning the handle and entering. Inside the passage she stood still and looked along its length. There was no one about and she walked to Tony Wayne's dressing room door and knocked.

'Come in,' he called and she entered.

He saw her in the mirror and turned in surprise.

'You!' he exclaimed.

'I'm sorry if I'm disturbing you,' she began nervously.

'You're not, Miss Manners,' he answered with a smile.

'How did you know my name?' she asked in surprise.

'Never mind that,' he said. 'What did you want to see me about?'

'I want to talk to you,' she said,

'privately. It's — it's rather urgent . . . '

'We can't talk privately here,' said Tony. 'Somebody's always dashing in and out.'

'Oh . . . It's really important,' she said.

'Can't I meet you somewhere later on?' he suggested. 'The matinée is nearly over.'

'Where?' she said doubtfully. 'All the places are so crowded.'

'Come back here,' he said. 'If you come back at six everybody will have gone and we'll have the place to ourselves.'

'Yes — all right — I'll do that,' she said.

'I'll wait for you,' said Tony.

Andy came rushing in almost knocking into her as she was about to leave.

'Have ye seen my nose?' he demanded. 'I must have left it . . . '

'Over there.' Tony pointed to a false nose on the dressing table. Andy picked it up.

'Fine,' he said and stopped as he saw the girl. Into his eyes came a startled look.

'I'll come back at six, Mr. Wayne,' she said and went out.

Andy stared after her;

'That was the girl,' he stammered. 'That was the girl . . . '

'I know,' said Tony.

'What did she want?'

'She didn't say. She'll tell me when she comes back.'

Andy carefully adjusted the false nose.

'Ye remember what happened the last time she was coming back?' he said seriously.

'I shall be here this time, Andy,' said Tony.

'Somebody was here last time,' said Andy. 'Only she didna come. It was the other poor woman.'

* * *

Superintendent Halliday laid down the report he had been reading and looked up at Detective-Sergeant Soames.

'McKay seems to be all right,' he said. 'There's nothing here. What about the other fellow, Gilbert?'

'Nothing through yet, sir,' said Soames. 'They don't seem to be able to trace him at all.'

'Because Gilbert isn't his name probably,' said Halliday. 'Did you manage to get hold of a photograph of him?'

'Yes, sir.' Soames nodded. 'I got that feller who takes snaps on the pier to catch him as he came off. I've had it blown up and sent to the Yard. It's quite a good likeness.'

'That may help.' Halliday rubbed his forehead. 'I'm sure there is something wrong about that chap. I've come up against him before, but for the life of me I can't think where. If only we could get a line on the dead woman.'

'Collins and Vance have drawn a blank up to now, sir.'

'She may have only just come down from London or somewhere,' said Halliday. 'If she hadn't been so badly injured we could have circulated a picture to the newspapers. Blasted nuisance.'

'We're checking up on the laundry marks, sir.'

'That all takes time,' said Halliday impatiently. 'We're stumped till we know who she was.'

'I still think McKay could help us, sir,' said Soames.

'You've got a bee in your bonnet about

133

McKay,' grunted the Superintendent irritably.

'Well, sir, he hasn't explained how that scrap of paper came to be found in her pocket,' answered Soames.

'It's always possible that he hasn't explained because he doesn't know,' said Halliday. 'We've got to concentrate on the woman's identity. If that ties up in any way with McKay we can have a go at him again.'

'It's a pity we couldn't find her hat and her handbag, sir,' remarked the Sergeant.

'If she had a hat,' said Halliday.

'She must have had a handbag, sir . . . '

'That's probably at the bottom of the sea somewhere.'

Soames cleared his throat.

'I've been wondering if it wouldn't be a good idea, sir, to get a diver on the job. Round about where the body was found. If we could find that handbag, sir . . . '

Halliday looked up at him alertly.

'That's a mighty good idea, Soames,' he said. 'Get to work on it at once, will you?'

'Yes, sir,' replied the gratified Sergeant.

'You don't know who took the packet?' said Jill Manners. She was sitting nervously on the edge of a chair facing Tony who had perched himself on the edge of the dressing table.

'I only know that when I looked for it, it had gone,' he replied. 'I suppose that's what you were doing here the other night — looking for it?'

'Yes, I — I found the door open. I didn't do any harm.' She looked at him appealingly. 'I was scared to death when you all came in. I hid on the stage.'

'I'm afraid you had all your trouble for nothing,' he said.

She nodded.

'I did,' she said ruefully.

'You might have got into serious trouble,' said Tony. 'What is there so valuable about this packet, Miss Manners?'

'I don't know,' she replied.

He looked at her incredulously.

'You don't know?' he repeated.

'No,' she answered. 'I was told that it

was very valuable, That's all. I was to deliver it to someone in Westpool . . . '

'Hargreaves?'

'You know?' she said in surprise.

'Who asked you to deliver it?' he said.

'Mr. Granger . . . '

'Is he a tall, thin man, with a scar on the left side of his face?'

'Do you know him?' she asked quickly.

'I know of him,' said Tony.

'He was injured during an air raid — that's how he came by the scar.'

'How are you connected with him?'

'I'm his secretary,' she answered. 'My father was one of his clients . . . '

'Clients?'

'Mr. Granger is a solicitor — Hargreaves and Granger. Mr. Hargreaves still has an interest in the firm, but he's retired . . . I don't know why I'm telling you all this . . . '

'Because you're very worried about something,' he said gently. 'Isn't that true?'

'Yes . . . I'm terribly worried,' she admitted.

'Why not tell me what's worrying you?'

he suggested. 'I might be able to help.'

She shook her head.

'It's very nice of you,' she said, 'but I'm afraid you couldn't.'

'May I suggest, Miss Manners,' interrupted the voice of Simon Beatal, 'that *I* could?'

She gave a startled little cry and turned to the door. The fat man was standing on the threshold. They had heard nothing. He must have opened the door very softly while they had been talking.

'Snooping again, Mr. Beatal?' said Tony.

Simon Beatal came in and closed the door behind him.

'An ugly word, sir,' he said, smiling blandly. 'I am here entirely in the interests of our mutual friend, Miss Manners.'

There was a frightened expression in her eyes as she stared at him.

'I — I don't know what you mean?' she said. 'How did you know I was here?'

'I followed you.'

'Following people seems to be a hobby of yours,' remarked Tony.

'Hardly a hobby, sir.' Simon Beatal

uttered one of his jerky little laughs. 'A matter of necessity, shall we say?'

'You were on the train,' said Jill, still staring at him fearfully. 'I — I was warned about you . . . '

'By Granger?' Simon Beatal nodded. 'I admit that I was following you on that occasion also.'

'Quite ubiquitous, aren't you?' said Tony.

'You might call it that, sir. Yes, it's a very apt description.'

'Well,' snapped Tony, 'suppose you try being ubiquitous somewhere else, Mr. Beatal.'

'If I adopted your suggestion, sir,' remarked Simon Beatal. 'I should leave Miss Manners suffering under a very grave injustice.'

'I don't suppose that would cause you to lose any sleep,' said Tony.

'You misjudge me, sir. I am a man of strong principles. I cannot remain silent and condone a swindle, sir.'

'Is this where we're supposed to laugh?' asked Tony.

Simon Beatal shook his head gravely.

'There is nothing humorous about it, sir,' he said. 'This charming young lady has been misled.'

'I don't understand,' said Jill.

'Naturally,' he answered indulgently. 'Certain things have been deliberately kept from you.'

'What do you mean?' she asked wonderingly.

'Would it surprise you to learn, Miss Manners,' he said, 'that potentially you are a very rich woman?'

'Rich?' She looked up at him in complete astonishment. 'Oh, you must be mistaken . . . '

'Your father, Miss Manners, made a very valuable discovery,' he said.

'My father is dead,' she answered. 'He was killed in a plane crash.'

'Exactly,' said Simon Beatal. 'And, if you'll forgive my saying so, that was the beginning of the trouble. Your father, Miss Manners, lived long enough to entrust his secret, together with certain proofs, to the pilot of the plane, with instructions that they were to be sent to his solicitor in England . . . '

'Is that what the packet contained?' broke in Tony interestedly.

'That, sir, is what the original packet contained,' agreed Simon Beatal.

'The original packet?' said Jill, frowning. 'I don't understand . . . '

'The packet that the pilot, before he too died of his injuries in the crash, succeeded in forwarding to Mr. Granger. The contents of that packet, Miss Manners, your father fully intended should be yours.'

'Are these more lies, Beatal?' said Tony.

'What I am telling Miss Manners, sir, are irrefutable facts.'

'But I had no idea that my — my father had sent anything,' said Jill.

'I am aware of that,' said Beatal. 'Cupidity, Miss Manners, gained the upper hand. Mr. Granger saw the opportunity of keeping an enormous fortune for himself. A lamentable decision.' He shook his head sadly.

'Which you were quite prepared to emulate, if you could have got hold of the packet,' remarked Tony.

'What was it my father discovered that

was so valuable?' asked Jill.

'I am a business man, Miss Manners,' answered Simon Beatal. 'I am not prepared to divulge that until I am sure that you are prepared to accept my proposition.'

Tony laughed.

'You're quite an adept at running with the fox and hunting with the hounds, aren't you?' he said admiringly.

'An excellent simile, sir,' said Beatal. 'If a trifle hackneyed. Hence the reason I am here at this moment. Let me assure you that whoever gets possession of the real packet, sir, need not give Miss Manners a single penny of its potential value. The mere possession of it is sufficient. Therefore, when I propose that Miss Manners should receive fifty per cent of the sum involved, I consider it to be a very generous offer, sir.'

'And a great deal more than you'd get if you had to cut up with Hargreaves, Granger and Renton?' said Tony sarcastically.

'You are shrewd, sir. That is, I admit, the main consideration.'

141

'You've got a nerve to offer her fifty per cent for something that you admit is all hers already!' said Tony.

'She would have difficulty in proving it, sir,' answered Simon Beatal. 'If you knew exactly what that packet contains, you would understand.'

'But you won't tell us that?'

'Not at the present stage of these negotiations, sir.'

'In fact,' said Tony, 'you're asking Miss Manners to buy a pig in a poke?'

'A very valuable pig, sir.'

'The snag is,' said Tony, 'that neither you nor Miss Masters have the slightest idea where the pig is.'

'Somebody stole the packet from Mr. Wayne's dressing room,' said Jill.

'That was not the *real* one, Miss Manners,' said Simon Beatal.

'That was taken from Vera Lee's digs,' said Tony.

Beatal laughed.

'A moot point, sir,' he said.

'You mean that was a dummy too?' asked Tony.

'In my opinion, sir,' said Simon Beatal.

Miss Masters was not the only one Mr. Granger was planning to — er — double-cross.'

'You mean — he's still got the original packet?' asked Tony.

'A reasonable supposition, sir,' replied the fat man, 'but not, I believe the correct one. It occurs to me that possibly Mr. Granger's wife knew its whereabouts . . . '

'Thelma?' asked Jill in surprise.

'Your sister, Miss Manners — your twin sister. Unfortunately she is not in a position to tell us.'

'Why do you say that?' asked Jill and there was sudden alarm in her voice. 'What's happened to her?'

'I regret very much to tell you that she's dead,' answered Simon Beatal gravely. 'She was murdered . . . '

11

It was late — the clock on the wall of the office showed the time to be nearly half-past ten, but Superintendent Halliday was still at his desk. He was frowning at a letter that Soames had just brought in to him.

'When did this come?' he asked, looking up.

'A few minutes ago,' answered the Sergeant. 'It was given to the station sergeant.'

'Who brought it?'

'A little thin-faced feller, so the sergeant says,' answered Soames. 'He said there wasn't any answer.'

'I'll bet he did,' grunted Halliday. 'Wish they'd detained him.'

'There was no reason to, sir,' said Soames.

Halliday read the letter again.

'If there's any truth in this somebody has saved us a lot of trouble,' he remarked. 'Listen.' He read the letter aloud. ''If you want to know who the dead woman was, ask Jill Manners. She lives in a caravan on the top of North Cliff'.'

'Whoever wrote that knows a bit too much, if you ask me,' said the Sergeant.

'It may be just one of the usual letters we get in a case like this,' said Halliday. 'Do you know anything about this caravan?'

'It must be on a private site, sir,' said Soames. 'There's no caravan colony or anything like that on North Cliff.'

'Get a car, Soames,' ordered Halliday, making up his mind. 'We'll go and find this woman, Jill Manners, and see if she knows anything.'

Soames glanced at the clock.

'It's a bit late, isn't it, sir?' said the Sergeant doubtfully. 'She may be in bed . . . '

'Then she'll have to get up,' snapped Halliday. 'We're going to follow this up right away.'

★ ★ ★

Renton poured himself a stiff whisky, gulped it down, and poured himself another. Hargreaves, pacing up and down the living room, stopped.

'I wouldn't have too much of that, if I were you,' he said.

'You mind your own business,' snapped Renton.

'I am,' said Hargreaves. 'You happen to be part of my business. Listen, I've been thinking . . . '

'There's a lot too much thinking,' retorted Renton. 'What we want is a little action.'

'You're going to get it,' said Hargreaves. 'I'm going out. I shan't be long.'

'Where are you going? It's nearly ten-thirty,' said Renton.

'I've got an idea where the packet is — the real one,' said Hargreaves. 'I'm going to see if I'm right.'

'Not without me you're not,' snapped Renton.

'You can't come . . . '

'Then you're not going,' declared Renton. He was slightly drunk and inclined to be more truculent than usual.

'Don't be a fool,' snarled Hargreaves.

'I'm not going to be, that's why I'm coming with you,' said Renton a little thickly. 'If you think I'm going to let you get hold of that packet without me, you'd better think some more.'

'What do you suppose I'm going to do?' demanded Hargreaves.

Renton smiled unpleasantly.

'I don't know,' he said, 'but whatever it is we're doing it together.'

'Look here, Renton . . . '

'What do you take me for, eh? Once you get your hands on that packet you'll clear out and I can whistle for my share until doomsday.'

'I wouldn't do that . . . '

'Not much you wouldn't. I'm taking no chances.'

'Very well, if you feel like that, you'd better come along,' said Hargreaves resignedly. 'But you'll do exactly as I tell you — understand?'

Renton nodded sullenly.

'Give me your gun,' said Hargreaves, holding out his hand.

'Nothing doing,' retorted Renton.

'Now, don't let's start another argument,' said Hargreaves. 'Either you give me that gun, or we don't go. I'll call the whole thing off. You can please yourself . . .'

Renton eyed him for a moment in silence. Then he pulled out the automatic and threw it on the table.

'There you are,' he snarled.

Hargreaves picked up the pistol and slipped it in his pocket.

'Good,' he said briefly. 'Now let's go . . .'

★ ★ ★

Jill Manners stubbed out her cigarette and began slowly to undress. It was comfortable inside the caravan if a trifle cramped for room. The hands of the small travelling clock on the table by the bed pointed to a quarter to eleven.

She looked worried and uneasy. She was thinking of her interview with Anthony Wayne and everything that Simon Beatal had said.

She got into bed and for a short while

she lay staring up at the low roof above her head.

She must have fallen asleep almost at once and how long she slept she didn't know, but she was awakened suddenly by a sound that for a moment she couldn't place. And then as she became wide awake she realised that it was somebody knocking at the door.

The knocking was repeated.

She got up and went over to the door.

'Who is it?' she called, her voice still husky with sleep.

A man's voice, muffled by the closed door, answered her.

'I've got an urgent message from Mr. Granger,' he called. 'It's very important . . . '

'Just a minute, please.' She put on the light and reached for her dressing gown. Going back to the door she turned the key and opened it. On the threshold stood the shadowy figure of a man. There was something wrapped round the lower part of his face but before she could see more he had pushed his way roughly into the caravan. She fell back with a startled cry as she saw the light glint on the automatic he held in a gloved hand.

'Be quiet!' he snapped curtly.

'Who are you?' she breathed fearfully.

'Never mind who I am,' he answered. 'Get back there and keep quiet. Then you won't be hurt . . . '

'What do you want?' she asked.

'The packet,' he said. 'I want the packet.'

'I — I haven't got it,' she stammered.

'It's here somewhere,' he retorted. 'Your sister hid it here.'

'My — my sister . . . ' Her eyes were frightened and her throat was so dry that the words were scarcely audible.

'Thelma Granger,' he said impatiently.

'But — she never had the packet.'

'How do you know?' he demanded quickly.

'She didn't — I'm — I'm sure she didn't . . . '

'I'm going to look. Keep quiet or it will be the worse for you.'

He began to make a thorough search while she watched him too terrified to move. Everything that could be moved he pulled out and thoroughly examined — books from the small shelf, cushions, the mattress and bedding on the narrow bed. Once when she thought he might not notice her, she began to edge towards the door but he swung quickly round on her.

'Don't try that,' he snarled threateningly. 'If you do you'll get hurt.'

There was something about the rough voice that did not ring true, she thought. A nuance that convinced her it was put on. And there was also something vaguely familiar about it. She was racking her brains to try and think why when the sound of a car came suddenly to her ears. The unknown man heard it too and stopped in his search to listen.

The car was approaching. It came nearer and stopped. A voice called to someone: 'This must be the place.' And another voice answered: 'There's a light, sir. She's still up.'

The man gripped Jill by the arm with a grip that made her wince.

'Keep quiet,' he whispered.

There came the sound of approaching

footsteps outside and then a knock on the door.

'Anyone by the name of Manners live here?' inquired a voice loudly.

The unknown man, pulling the girl after him, moved over to the door softly.

'Hello there. We're from the police. We'd like a word with you,' called the voice.

'Tell them you're coming,' whispered the man with his lips close to her ear.

'I'm coming,' she called obediently and a little quaveringly.

'All right, miss,' came the answer. 'Sorry to disturb you but it's important.'

The unknown man motioned her to get on the other side of the door. As she did so he suddenly flung the door open and dashed out. Clutching the door frame for support she heard a startled cry from outside followed by the sound of a shot.

'Look out, Soames,' cried the voice that had spoken before. 'Grab him — he's got a gun.'

There came the sound of another shot farther away and a faint cry. There was a confused noise of shouting.

Halliday came quickly up the steps and into the caravan.

'Is your name Jill Manners?' he asked as he saw the frightened girl crouching back against the wall.

'Yes,' she answered faintly.

'Who was the man who just left here?' he asked.

'I — I don't know . . . '

'What did he want? How did he get in?' demanded Halliday.

'He — he said he had a message for me . . . I let him in,' she stammered. 'Are you — are you from the police?'

'I'm Superintendent Halliday of the Westpool C.I.D.,' said Halliday. 'I'm inquiring into the death of an unknown woman whose body was found in the sea off the pier. From certain information that has come into my possession, I believe you may be able to identify the dead woman.'

Soames came in before she could reply. He was breathless and there was a nasty gash across his right wrist.

'He got away, sir,' he said.

Holliday uttered an exclamation.

'You're hurt, man,' he cried.

'It's only a scratch,' said the Sergeant. 'One of the shots grazed my wrist.'

'Let me look,' said Halliday. 'It's a nasty gash. Have you got anything I can bind this up with?' He turned to the girl.

'I — I think my sister kept a first-aid box in the kitchen,' she said shakily. 'I'll go and look.'

She moved unsteadily towards the narrow opening that led into the tiny kitchen. Halliday looked after her.

'Her sister,' he whispered to Soames. 'I think that note we got was genuine, after all.'

12

Simon Beatal was sitting in an easy chair in the sitting room of his suite in the Majestic Hotel placidly reading a novel. It was quite late but he was comfortably clad in a silken dressing gown and there was a decanter of brandy on a small table by his side. The book he was reading was a popular love romance by that prolific and somewhat cloying writer, Miss Rachel Sweeting. Simon Beatal was partial to that type of story.

The house telephone near his elbow buzzed softly and with a frown he laid aside his book and picked up the receiver.

'Yes?' he said and a moment later: 'Send him up.'

After a little while Chives came in.

'It's a bit late but I thought I'd better come,' he said.

'The lateness of the hour means nothing to me, sir,' said Simon Beatal. 'When there is business to be discussed I am available at any time. What exactly is it you wish to tell me?'

'Did you know that girl 'as got a caravan — up on North Cliff?' asked Chives.

'Miss Manners? Come, come, sir, I hope you did not put yourself to all this trouble just to tell me something I already knew?'

'Not altogether,' said Chives. 'Hargreaves an' Renton 'ave just gone up there.'

'To the caravan?'

'Yes. That's why I came. I thought you'd want to know.'

'You were quite right, sir,' said Simon Beatal.

'Did the estimable Mr. Granger go with them?'

Chives shook his head.

'No — only the two of 'em,' he said.

'Things seem to be moving, sir,' remarked Beatal.

'What do you think they're up to?' asked the little man.

'When people are acting at cross purposes — I might almost say double-cross purposes — it is very difficult to say what they are up to, sir.'

'What are you going to do about it?' said Chives.

'I, sir, am going to finish this excellent novel and I retire to my bed,' said Simon Beatal. 'I have reached a certain conclusion on my course of action, sir. It will, I believe, not only give a severe shock to people of our acquaintance, but prove exceedingly advantageous to myself.' He laughed and picked up his book. 'I wish you good night, sir.'

He settled himself comfortably in his chair and went on reading.

★ ★ ★

'Now let me get this clear, Miss Manners,' said Superintendent Halliday. 'You came down to Westpool on the Sunday for the purpose of delivering a supposedly valuable parcel to a certain Mr. Wilson Hargreaves. The parcel having been entrusted to you by your employer, Mr. Granger?'

'That's quite right,' said the girl.

They were sitting in the small room in

157

the caravan. Sergeant Soames had had the wound in his wrist bound up and Halliday had been questioning the girl.

'On the journey down, you became aware that you were being followed by a man called Simon Beatal, whom you had been warned might make an attempt to get the parcel,' continued Halliday. 'In a sudden panic you threw the parcel into a compartment on the train in which certain members of The Crimson Ramblers concert party were travelling, having scribbled a message on it that you would call for it at the Dome. What made you choose that particular compartment?'

'They were the only people on the train I knew I could find again,' she answered. 'I'd seen their luggage on the platform. I knew they were going to the Dome Pavilion.'

Halliday smiled.

'As simple as that, eh?' he said. 'Now, let me see what else you've told me. You had to wait until Monday before you could contact these concert party people so you decided to stay the night at this caravan, which belonged to your father, and to which both you and your sister had keys. Right?

'You couldn't collect the parcel when you called at the Dome Pavilion on Monday afternoon, because Mr. Wayne had left it at his lodgings,' Halliday went on. 'You arranged to call back again in the evening. When you got back here, you found that your sister, Mrs. Granger, had arrived during your absence. Let's go on from there, Miss Manners. Did she tell you what had brought her to Westpool?'

The girl shook her head.

'No, but she seemed rather excited about something and rather surprised and annoyed that I should have turned up,' she said. 'I didn't take much notice of that. Thelma and I never hit it off very well and we hadn't seen each other for months.'

'Didn't she ever come to the office — her husband's office?' asked Halliday.

'Oh, no,' she replied. 'You see, they weren't — well, friendly. I don't think she's seen him for — oh, goodness knows how long.'

'I see,' remarked Halliday thoughtfully.

'Did you tell her about the parcel?'

'Yes — and I thought she behaved very queerly,' said the girl.

'How do you mean — queerly?' asked Halliday quickly.

'She asked me if I knew what was in it, and when I said 'no' she laughed. I said I couldn't see anything to laugh at and she said: 'You wouldn't — not even if you knew'.'

'Did she give you the impression that she knew?' asked Halliday.

'I don't know. I didn't really take much notice. You see, I had a splitting headache and I really did feel ill. All I wanted to do was to lie down and keep quiet.'

'I know the kind,' said the Superintendent sympathetically. 'I have 'em myself sometimes.'

'Like a really fierce hangover,' remarked Sergeant Soames feelingly.

'You probably know more about that than we do,' snapped Halliday.

'Thelma was quite nice about it,' the girl went on, 'which in itself was a bit unusual. She made me some tea, told me to lie down, and offered to go to the Dome,

160

instead of me, and collect the packet.'

'Did she go?'

'Yes. She said that if she put on my clothes nobody who didn't know us very well, would notice the difference.'

'A black suit?' asked Halliday with interest.

'Yes. How did you . . . ' She suddenly realised how he did know and her face went white.

'Was there a scrap of paper in one of the pockets with the name 'McKay' on it?' said Halliday.

She frowned.

'I don't know . . . That's the name of the man who runs the concert party, isn't it? Oh, yes, I remember. I scribbled his name down when I got to Westpool, so that I'd know who to ask for.'

'That clears that up.' Halliday shot a quick glance at Soames. 'Surely, Miss Manners, when your sister didn't come back, you must have thought there was something wrong?'

'I was worried . . . but it was so like Thelma. I thought she'd just cleared off back to London.'

'Didn't you telephone Mr. Granger?'

'I'd already done that — first thing on the Monday morning,' she explained. 'I told him what had happened to the packet. He told me not to worry. He said I'd soon get it back again.'

'Didn't that strike you as rather a casual way to treat the loss of something that was supposed to be very valuable? You didn't know then that the packet was a fake, did you?'

'I suppose I was too relieved that he hadn't made a fuss to think much about it,' she said.

'You haven't been in communication with Mr. Granger since?' asked the Superintendent.

She shook her head.

'So he doesn't know that your sister came down here?'

'Not from me,' she said.

Halliday frowned thoughtfully and stroked his chin.

'From what this man, Beatal, told you,' he said after a pause, 'Granger was trying to appropriate something of considerable value which your father had discovered and which was rightly yours. Would your sister have shared in it?'

'I don't know,' answered the girl. 'I've no idea what it could be.'

'What was your father's business, Miss Manners?'

'He hadn't any,' she answered and smiled. 'I mean he'd tried all sorts of things. Some of them made money — some didn't. The last time I saw him he was practically broke.'

'You don't know what he was doing in Canada when he was killed?'

Again she shook her head.

'No,' she replied. 'As a matter of fact I didn't even know he was in Canada until Mr. Granger told me he had been killed in a plane crash.'

'Whereabouts did that happen?'

'Near Saskatchewan, I believe.'

'That man who was here when we arrived, Miss Manners,' said Halliday. 'You said he thought your sister had the real packet and had hidden it here?'

'That's what he said. I'm quite certain she didn't.'

Halliday rose to his feet.

'We'd better make sure,' he said. 'It won't take long to search this place. If she did have the packet — and somebody knew it — we can guess the motive for her murder.'

★ ★ ★

Hargreaves paced restlessly about the living room at the bungalow, his chin on his chest, his thin hands clasped behind his back.

Renton leaned up against the mantelpiece, staring with growing irritability at his companion.

'For Pete's sake stop the tiger act!' he burst out at last. 'It's getting on my nerves.'

'How did the police find out about Jill,' muttered Hargreaves, continuing his ceaseless patrol round the room.

'Does it matter?' snapped Renton. 'All that matters is that your little party was a complete fiasco.'

'How was I to know the police would turn up?' said Hargreaves.

'It's a lucky thing we're not both in

clink,' said Renton. 'You winged one of 'em.'

'It was the only way — he nearly caught me.'

'All that trouble,' snarled Renton disgustedly, 'and we're no nearer getting the packet than we were before.'

'I still think it's hidden in the caravan,' said Hargreaves.

'Fat lot of good to us that is,' grunted Renton. 'We can't take the place to pieces. Maybe Beatal can suggest something.'

'I don't trust Beatal . . . '

'I don't trust anybody — not even you,' said Renton. 'What's Granger up to tonight?'

'I haven't seen him.'

'No, he went out early this evening and he hasn't come back. It's nearly one o'clock. What's he up to?'

'I don't know . . . '

'More double-crossing, I suppose,' said Renton crossly.

'If only we could lay our hands on that packet and clear out,' said Hargreaves. 'We wouldn't have to bother about any of them then.'

'If, if, if,' sneered Renton. 'The whole

165

of this business has been nothing but if. We should never have left this to Granger in the first place. I said so right from the start but you had to be pig-headed. All this nonsense of sending the packet down here. We ought to have gone up to London and collected it ourselves . . . '

'You know why we didn't?' retorted Hargreaves. 'With Beatal watching like a cat at a mousehole we'd have been spotted at once. We'd never have got away with it. Granger thought that if he sent Jill Manners as a decoy and got the other girl to bring the real packet, it would be safe.'

'And now look what's happened?' grunted Renton. 'If you ask me, Granger worked it out very well.'

'You think Beatal's right?'

'Yes, I do. You can say what you like about it being hidden in the caravan but I believe Granger's got it. If I had my way I'd rough him up until we got the truth.'

'I object to violence . . . '

'You didn't object to shooting that copper.'

'That was unavoidable.'

'You're too squeamish. Unless you

want to lose a fortune you'd better try a little violence with Granger.'

Hargreaves shook his head.

'There are other ways of dealing with Granger,' he said.

'You tell me one as good,' said Renton.

'I'll tell you one that's better,' answered Hargreaves. He came over and sat down. 'Listen . . . '

For nearly twenty minutes he talked softly and Renton listened, his small eyes glistening with approval as Hargreaves outlined his plan.

13

Andy had called a rehearsal for the morning following the events in the caravan on North Cliff. It was a little after ten o'clock that the company at the Dome Pavilion waiting for Andy's arrival.

'I do hope,' said Sharon, 'that Andy won't keep us long this morning. I've got a lot of shopping to do.'

'I don't know what he wanted to call a rehearsal at all for,' said Vera a trifle crossly. 'Everything's going quite well.'

'It's for the new numbers,' explained Beryl.

'We've done the new numbers,' said Vera.

'We need quite a lot you know,' said Billy. 'Andy's idea is to change the show as often as possible. You can get the same people in twice that way.'

'Trust Andy to think of something like that,' said Vera.

'Well, dear,' put in Beryl gently. 'He's

not running the show for fun, you know.'

'Of course, you would stick up for him,' snapped Vera.

'I don't see why he had to call all of us,' said Sharon.

'Well, Tony's not here — neither is Gilbert,' remarked Billy.

'Nor Andy,' said Vera. 'He's usually the first.'

'I think we're a bit early,' said Beryl.

'Funny how Gilbert's managed to stay so unfriendly, isn't it?' said Billy. 'Keeps himself very much to himself.'

'That's something to be thankful for,' said Vera feelingly.

'Who's the little thin-faced man he's always talking to?' asked Sharon. 'Anybody know?'

'What little man?' asked Billy.

'Haven't you seen him?' said Sharon. 'I've seen them together several times. They always seem to be lurking in doorways.'

'I suppose Gilbert's got to talk to somebody now and again,' said Billy.

'So long as it isn't me,' said Vera, 'I don't mind. I don't like the man.'

'We rather gathered that, darling,' remarked Billy.

Andy came in the stage door rubbing his hands.

'Good morning everybody,' he greeted cheerfully. 'I see ye're all here eager to get to work.'

'I don't know about 'eager', Andy,' said Sharon. 'I was just saying I hoped you weren't going to keep us long.'

'I'll no keep ye longer than I can help,' said Andy. 'I want to put the new numbers into the show at the matinée next Monday.'

Tony came in quickly.

'I say, I'm not late, am I?' he asked.

'No,' answered Andy. 'I've only just arrived myself. Let's go up on the stage and get started.'

He set off along the passage towards the stage.

'Did you call Gilbert?' asked Billy as they followed him.

'Aye,' said Andy. 'Is he no here yet?!'

'We haven't seen him,' said Vera.

'Well, we'll start without him,' said Andy.

Sharon was last as the others went up the steps to the stage, and Tony dropped back to her side.

'Sharon,' he began, but she moved away quickly.

'Listen,' he said in a low voice, 'I want to talk to you . . . '

'I'm in a hurry,' she answered coldly.

'Look here,' he urged, 'why are you being so pig-headed?'

She turned and gave him a devastating stare.

'I wish you wouldn't keep annoying me,' she said, and hurried on up the steps.

The passage remained empty for a minute or two after they had all gone and then Howard Gilbert came in the stage door and went straight to his dressing room. Again the passage was empty but not for long. The stage door began to open slowly and a distorted shadow was flung along the wall by the brilliant sunshine outside. The shadow moved, and grew larger as somebody slipped inside the stage door. And then it vanished as the door was closed . . .

In the living room at Hargreaves' bungalow, on that sunny morning, there was a discussion in progress between Granger, Renton, and Hargreaves.

It was not an amicable discussion to judge from the expressions on the faces of the three men.

'Why start this all over again?' demanded Granger. 'I thought we'd thrashed it out once.'

'Wishful thinking, Granger,' said Renton. 'I still believe you've got that packet stowed away somewhere, or you know where it is.'

'I've already told you . . .' began Granger angrily.

'We're not satisfied, Granger,' said Hargreaves.

'That's a pity, isn't it?' snapped Granger unpleasantly.

'You may find it so,' said Renton.

'What do you mean?' Granger swung round on him.

'Do you remember that business of old Nesbitt, three years ago?' asked Hargreaves.

Granger started.

'Yes, I remember it,' he answered uneasily. 'Why bring it up now?'

'You could have got five years for that, Granger,' said Hargreaves. 'You could *still* get five years.'

'You were in it too,' said Granger.

'You'd have difficulty in proving that, I think,' replied Hargreaves smoothly.

'What are you getting at?' Granger looked at him sharply.

'I'm merely advising you to tell us the truth,' said Hargreaves coolly. 'Where is the packet — the real packet — that David Manners arranged to be sent to you before he died?'

'I've told you — I don't know . . . '

'Think again,' said Renton. 'Five years is a long time.'

Granger's face hardened but there was an expression of fear in his eyes.

'I see,' he said. 'Blackmail — is that it?'

'That's it,' agreed Renton. 'Now, let's have the truth . . . '

At that moment there was a sound of a bell. It was followed by a loud knocking on the front door.

'Who the devil can that be?' muttered

Hargreaves, frowning.

'I'll go,' said Renton curtly.

He left the room and they heard him open the door.

'Mr. Hargreaves?' inquired an official voice.

'What do you want?' asked Renton's voice.

'I'm Detective-Superintendent Halliday of the Westpool C.I.D.,' answered the voice that had spoken before. 'I want to see Mr. Hargreaves.'

Hargreaves uttered an exclamation and his face went white.

'Just a minute,' said Renton.

He came quickly into the room and shut the door.

'It's the police,' he whispered.

Hargreaves nodded.

'We heard,' he said.

'What shall I do?' asked Renton. 'Do you think it's about last night?'

'No.' Hargreaves shook his head. 'They couldn't identify either of us . . . '

'What do you mean — last night?' put in Granger

'Nothing to do with you,' snapped

Renton. 'What are you going to do?'

'See them, of course,' answered Hargreaves. 'What have we got to worry about?' He had recovered from his momentary shock. He went over to the door and called: 'Come in.'

Halliday entered followed by Soames. Hargreaves noticed that the Sergeant's wrist was bandaged. This must be the man he had wounded.

'Do you want to see me privately?' he asked genially. 'These gentlemen are friends of mine — Mr. Renton — Mr. Granger.'

Halliday looked from one to the other as he introduced them.

'Mr. Granger, eh?' he said. 'Well, now, that's going to save us a lot of trouble, sir. I've been trying to get hold of you on the telephone.'

'What for?' asked Granger quickly.

'It concerns your wife, sir,' said Halliday.

'Thelma!' exclaimed Granger.

Halliday nodded.

'I'm afraid I've some bad news for you, sir,' he said.

Hargreaves and Renton exchanged glances.

'Bad news?' said Granger. 'I don't understand . . . '

'On Tuesday last,' said Halliday, 'the dead body of a woman was found in the sea. It has been identified by Miss Jill Manners as being that of her sister . . . '

'Good God!' Granger looked horrified. 'How did it happen? Who killed her?'

'I never suggested that it was a question of murder,' said Halliday quietly.

Granger was a little disconcerted.

'You said . . . ' he began.

'I said 'the dead body of a woman had been found in the sea',' said Halliday.

'Well, I thought . . . naturally I concluded that . . . ' Granger stopped rather confused by the Superintendent's steady stare.

'That it was murder, sir? That's rather curious. It might have been an accident.'

'Was it?' asked Granger.

'No, sir,' answered Halliday. 'You were quite right, as it happens. Death was due to strangulation.'

'Good heavens — this is dreadful

news,' put in Hargreaves.

Halliday turned his steady gaze on him.

'Is it entirely news to you, Mr. Hargreaves?' he asked.

'I'd heard that a woman's body had been found but, naturally, I never connected it with Mrs. Granger,' said Hargreaves easily. 'Do you know who killed her?'

'That's what we're trying to discover, sir,' said Halliday. 'I'm hoping that you will be able to help us.'

'Do you mind if I have a drink,' said Granger shakily. 'This — this has rather upset me.'

He went over to the table and poured himself out a large whisky. The hand holding the bottle was shaking.

'Why should you imagine that we can help you?' asked Hargreaves.

'I think I ought to tell you,' interrupted Granger. 'That for a long time my wife and I have not been on very friendly terms.'

He gulped down the neat whisky and a little colour came back to his face.

Halliday nodded.

'So I understand from Miss Manners, he said. 'When did you last see your wife?'

Granger frowned in an effort of memory.

'I can't tell you exactly,' he answered after a pause, with a great air of frankness. 'It's quite a considerable time now.'

'I see.' Halliday's face was expressionless. 'I believe her father was killed in a plane crash near Saskatchewan a short time ago.'

He noted with inward satisfaction the consternation that was depicted on the three faces before him.

'Her father . . . ' repeated Granger in a husky voice.

'David Manners,' said Halliday pleasantly.

'Yes . . . that's — that's true,' said Granger after a pause.

'Just prior to his death he made a very valuable discovery of some kind, didn't he?' Halliday went on remorselessly. 'Can you give me any information concerning that?'

Granger passed his tongue over dry lips.

'A valuable discovery?' he repeated.

'That's news to me. I'm afraid I don't know anything about that.'

'Would you like to reconsider that answer, sir?' invited the Superintendent. 'Of course, you're not under oath . . . '

'What do you mean?' Granger tried to bluster. 'Look here, you've no right to ask all these questions . . . '

'You're not bound to answer them, sir, I'll admit,' said Halliday. 'Do I understand that you refuse to answer my questions?' He looked over at Soames. 'Will you witness that, Sergeant?' he added.

'Yes, sir,' replied Soames smartly.

'Look here,' interposed Hargreaves, 'there's no need to take that attitude, Superintendent. We are prepared to help you all we can. Naturally, as members of the legal profession, we are aware that you cannot enforce us to answer, but . . . '

'Quite so, sir,' answered Halliday. 'According to our information, details concerning the discovery made by David Manners were sent to Mr. Granger by the pilot of the plane. He afterwards died from his injuries in hospital. Is that correct?'

'Where did you get this information?' inquired Hargreaves.

'I should be glad if you would answer the question, sir,' said Halliday.

'I understood,' interpolated Granger, 'that you were investigating the death of my wife. What's all this got to do with that?'

'I believe it was the motive for the murder,' said Halliday. 'You affirm, do you, sir, that you know nothing about any valuable discovery made by David Manners?'

Granger nodded.

'I know nothing about it at all,' he declared.

'You didn't decide to appropriate it for yourself although it belonged to Miss Manners?'

'You've no right to make accusations like that,' said Hargreaves.

'I haven't made any accusations — yet, sir,' answered the Superintendent. 'I only asked a question . . .'

'And I've answered it,' broke in Granger. 'I don't know what you're talking about.'

Halliday turned to Soames.

'Fetch Mr. Simon Beatal in, will you?' he ordered.

'Beatal!' cried Hargreaves sharply.

'He's waiting outside in the car,' said Halliday. 'I think what he has to say will make you change your mind, Mr. Granger.'

★ ★ ★

Vera came to the end of her new number and waited for the approval or otherwise of Andy who was sitting in the front row of the stalls.

'That's no too bad,' he called up to her. 'Ye can maybe slow up a wee bit before the end. We'll leave it now,' he added. 'Where's Gilbert?'

'I'll go and fetch him,' volunteered Tony.

'Aye — and tell him to hurry up, we're waiting,' said Andy. 'He should have come up on the stage with the rest of ye.'

'Perhaps he hasn't come in?' said Billy.

'If he's no there,' called Andy, 'tell him I'll have a lot to say to him when he is.'

Tony laughed and hurried away. He ran down the steps and along the passage. He tapped on the door of Gilbert's dressing room but there was no reply.

Tony opened the door and put his head inside.

'I say, Gilbert,' he called to the man who was sitting in the chair before the dressing table. 'You're holding up rehearsal . . . '

But there was no answer or movement from the figure in the chair.

'Hi!' called Tony. 'Are you asleep?'

He went over and put his hand on the man's shoulder. The next second he was back in the passage, his face white and strained.

'Andy,' he shouted, 'Andy . . . Andy, for God's sake come here — quickly . . . '

Billy came running.

'What is it?' he called. 'What's the matter?'

'It's Gilbert . . . Fetch Andy, will you?'

But Andy had heard and came hurriedly in through the pass door.

'What are ye shouting about?' he demanded.

'It's Gilbert — he's dead,' said Tony.

'Dead?' echoed Billy.

'Yes,' said Tony. 'Come and look . . . '

He led the way back along the passage to Gilbert's room. The rest of the company came crowding down the steps from the stage.

'You'd better keep the girls away,' said Tony. 'It's not very pleasant.'

'What was it — a heart attack?' asked Billy.

'No — he's been strangled,' answered Tony.

14

Simon Beatal came slowly into the living room followed by Soames. If looks could have killed he would have dropped down dead in the doorway from the venom that was directed at him from three pairs of eyes.

'Now, Mr. Granger,' said Halliday. 'I should advise you to tell the whole truth about this business. I don't think you realise what a serious position you may find yourself in if you don't.'

'I've got you to thank for this,' snarled Granger, glaring at the fat man.

'Not at all, sir,' said Simon Beatal smoothly. 'I merely acted in accordance with the dictates of my conscience.'

'Conscience!' shouted Renton. 'Why you double-crossing swine . . . '

He made a quick movement towards the fat man but Halliday checked him.

'Now, now,' he said sharply. 'We'll have none of that.'

'Be quiet, Renton,' snapped Hargreaves. 'This man's word is not to be relied upon, Superintendent,'

'That seems to apply to all of you,' said Halliday.

'Beatal was as much in this as anybody,' grated Renton. 'He . . . '

'*Will* you be quiet,' cut in Hargreaves.

'Mr. Beatal may be in it or he may not,' said Halliday. 'All I'm interested in at present is a statement from Mr. Granger.'

'I suppose I've no option,' said Granger. He shot a malignant glance at Simon Beatal.

'I ought to warn you that anything you say will be taken down in writing and may be used in evidence hereafter,' said Halliday.

'I wondered if you were going to remember that, Superintendent,' said Hargreaves.

'I've done nothing criminal,' said Granger.

'We none of us have,' added Hargreaves quickly.

'What do you call entering into a conspiracy with intent to defraud?' asked Halliday.

'That doesn't apply to me, sir,' said

Simon Beatal. 'Miss Manners can assure you of that.'

'You great fat slug!' cried Renton furiously. 'You make me sick.'

'The court will decide who it applies to,' said Halliday impatiently. 'I want to know what it was that David Manners found.'

'I can tell you that, sir,' said the fat man. 'In one word. Uranium!'

'Uranium!' repeated Halliday.

'A very valuable substance, sir, in these enlightened days,' remarked Simon Beatal. 'Worth more than gold — and infinitely more dangerous. The basis of our atomic age, sir . . .'

'Cut out the lecture,' snarled Renton.

'David Manners found a quantity of this stuff?' asked Halliday.

'He stumbled on one of the largest uranium strikes that has ever been discovered,' said Granger. 'In a tract of unexplored country beyond Lake Athabaska in Northern Saskatchewan. The only way to reach the area is by plane.'

'I suppose it would be very valuable?' said Halliday.

'Valuable!' Hargreaves laughed harshly. 'It's worth several fortunes . . . '

'A great temptation, sir.' Simon Beatal shook his head sorrowfully. 'You must admit that few could resist such an opportunity if it was within their grasp.'

'That depends on how you look at it,' said Halliday shortly. 'Every bank is a great temptation to a burglar. What was in the packet that was sent you, Mr. Granger?'

'A map and photographs of the exact location,' answered Granger. 'There was also a covering letter from the pilot and a note from David Manners to me.'

'What did that say?' asked Halliday.

'It was difficult to read — he must have been dying when he wrote it. It asked me to register the claim in the name of — Jill Manners.'

'I see,' said Halliday. 'But anybody who was in possession of the map and the photographs could register the claim in their own name?'

'Yes.'

There was a world of contempt in Halliday's eyes as he regarded Granger.

'That is what you intended to do?' he said. 'Without telling Miss Manners anything about it?'

'It was too big an operation for a young girl to handle, Superintendent,' said Hargreaves. 'You must see that.'

'The only thing I see,' retorted Halliday, 'is that this property was rightfully Miss Manners'. Nobody else has any right to it at all. Now, where is this packet with the map and the photographs?'

'It was stolen from Miss Lee's lodgings,' said Granger promptly.

'I understand that was a dummy packet,' said the Superintendent.

'Then you understand more than I do,' retorted Granger.

'Come, come, sir,' interposed Simon Beatal. 'Why not admit the truth? The time for dissembling is past . . . '

'Why don't you shut up?' cried Renton.

'It's my opinion that the real packet was in the possession of your wife, Mr. Granger,' said Halliday.

'How could she have got hold of it?'

'I don't know how she got it, but I

believe it was in her possession,' persisted Halliday. 'I believe it was the reason she was murdered.'

There was a sudden loud ringing at the front door bell and a thunderous rat-tat-tat on the knocker. 'Now what is it?' cried Hargreaves.

'Go and see who it is, Soames,' ordered Halliday and the Sergeant went quickly out.

The front door opened, there was a hurried murmur of voices, and then Soames reappeared followed by Chives. The little man was excited and almost incoherent.

'Can you come to the Dome?' he panted, catching Halliday by the arm. 'There's been another murder . . . '

'Who is it?' demanded the Superinten-dent.

'Ex-Inspector John Howard,' said Chives. ''E was appearing in the concert party under the name of 'Oward Gilbert.'

★　★　★

Outside the stage door at the Dome Pavilion a uniformed constable stood on guard. Inside, grouped together uneasily, were the members of the concert party, with the exception of Sharon who had gone earlier before the grim discovery, and the dead man who still sat in his chair behind the closed door of the dressing room. By himself, leaning against the wall and staring at the floor, stood Chives.

There had been great activity following the arrival of Superintendent Halliday and Soames. Photographers and finger-print men had come and gone and the police surgeon had made his examination. Behind the closed door Halliday and Soames were conducting the preliminary investigation into the murder.

They had taken statements from all the company but had refused permission for any of them to leave the building.

'Isn't this awful, Andy,' said Beryl, her usually smiling face grave and serious. 'There's been nothing but trouble since we came here. First that woman and now this.'

Andy nodded. He looked worried and depressed.

'Aye,' he said, 'there's been trouble enough. I'll be glad to see the last of it.'

Vera sighed.

'How much longer do you think they'll keep us hanging about here?' she asked.

Tony shrugged his shoulders.

'There's no knowing,' he answered.

'We've told them all we know about it,' said Billy.

'Which isna much,' said Andy.

'I think they might let us go,' said Beryl. 'What can they want to keep us hanging about here for?'

'Further questioning, I suppose,' said Tony.

'But we can't tell them anything more,' she said.

'I promised to meet Sharon for a swim,' said Billy. 'She'll be wondering what's happened to me . . . '

'You'd better tell Superintendent Halliday,' said Vera, 'perhaps it will hurry him up.'

'I suppose it's all wrong,' sighed Beryl, 'but I'm getting terribly hungry.'

'If ye miss your lunch it'll be good for your figure,' said Andy.

'Andy,' she exclaimed. 'Are you beginning to notice my figure at last?'

'Ye canna miss it!' retorted Andy.

'Andy!' she cried indignantly. 'Anybody would think I was fat.'

'Plump, dear, plump,' said Billy. 'It sounds better.'

They were trying to infuse a little brightness into the gloom that had descended on them. But it was only momentary. The knowledge of that closed door and what lay behind it could not be kept at bay.

'I wonder what they're doing in there all this time?' said Vera after a short silence.

'They haven't been very long, you know,' said Tony.

'It seems ages,' said Vera. 'Sharon was lucky to have got away before it happened. I wish I had.'

'We don't know exactly when it did happen, do we?' said Tony.

'It could have been any time after we started rehearsal,' remarked Andy.

'Or even before,' put in Billy. 'We don't know what time Gilbert got here.'

He fumbled in his pocket, took out a cigarette and lighted it.

Vera gave a sudden shiver.

'It's horrible,' she said. 'Two murders . . . '

'And it looks as if they were both committed by the same person,' said Tony thoughtfully.

'It's rather frightening — to think that there's someone going around strangling people,' said Beryl.

'Don't talk about it,' said Vera sharply.

'It's even more frightening when ye realise that it may be someone we know,' said Andy.

They stared at him.

'What do you mean?' asked Billy.

'Don't joke about it,' said Vera.

'I was never more serious in my life,' declared Andy.

'But, Andy . . . you don't think . . . you can't mean . . . ' Beryl was slightly incoherent and her eyes were scared. 'You can't mean — one of *us*?'

'Aye,' said Andy seriously. 'It might be.'

* * *

The ambulance came and all that remained of Howard Gilbert, or to give him his real name, John Howard, was removed on a stretcher. The news of the murder had spread and a crowd of holidaymakers watched the body, covered with a blanket, carried to the waiting ambulance at the entrance to the pier.

In the dressing room that the dead man had occupied, Halliday, perched on the edge of the dressing table, frowned at Soames.

'Well,' he said, 'we've got all the preliminary statements and it boils down to this. Any three of 'em could have done it — McKay, Wayne or Dale. They all left the stage on one pretext or another during rehearsal this morning.'

'And the women, sir,' said Soames. 'They weren't on the stage all the time.'

Halliday nodded.

'That's right,' he agreed. 'I suppose we can't rule them out entirely. It wouldn't have required a great deal of strength . . . '

'Women are pretty strong these days, sir,' said the Sergeant. 'Now my wife . . . '

'We know it wasn't her,' interrupted

194

Halliday. 'It's possible someone came in from outside . . . '

'That girl, Sharon Roy, left early, sir,' said Soames. 'She could have come back.'

'Why should she want to kill Howard?' demanded Halliday. 'He was killed by the same person who strangled Thelma Granger.'

'Well, sir,' said the Sergeant, 'perhaps she killed her too.'

'What for?' said Halliday impatiently. 'She was killed because of this uranium business . . . '

'Miss Roy may be mixed up in that, sir,' persisted Soames,

'She may, but I doubt it,' answered Halliday. 'No wonder Gilbert looked familiar to me, he added. 'Of course, I remember him now. He was on the Drayton case — a nasty business. What the dickens he was doing here, I can't imagine.'

'That feller, Chives, might give us a line there, sir.'

Halliday nodded.

'We'll have him in,' he said. 'Call him, will you?'

Soames went over to the door and called: 'Mr. Chives.'

Chives came in.

'Shut the door,' said Halliday crisply. 'Now, will you tell us what ex-Detective Inspector was doing masquerading as a singer in this concert party?'

'He was workin' on a job,' answered Chives promptly. 'When he retired from the police 'e opened a private agency.'

'So he was running a private agency, eh?' said Hallliday. 'I suppose you were working for him. Is that right?'

'That's right, I was 'is assistant,' said Chives.

'What job was he on here?' asked Halliday.

''E was workin' for the Schiller Minin' Company,' said Chives.

'The Schiller Mining Company,' repeated Halliday. 'Anything to do with — uranium?'

'You know about that, do you?' said Chives.

'A little — I'd like to know a lot more. Had this company got anything to do with David Manners?'

Chives nodded.

'The Schiller Company financed Manners,' he replied. 'Manners crashed in a plane an' . . . '

'I know all about that,' broke in the Superintendent.

'Well, after the crash, this minin' company got wind that Manners 'ad struck lucky,' said Chives.

'How?'

'It's a long story,' began Chives but Halliday interrupted him.

'Just give me the bare details now,' he said. 'We can go into the full story later.'

'It was the pilot of the plane,' explained Chives. ' 'E was badly hurt in the crash an' taken to 'ospital. Towards the end 'e got delirious. One o' the nurses in the 'ospital was friendly with a girl who worked in the Schiller Company an' she told this girl what she'd 'eard this feller mutterin' about in 'is delirium. Manners 'ad 'ad an agreement with the Schiller Company an' they thought they ought to 'ave a cut in what 'e'd found. But they didn't know what had 'appened to the maps an' things. They got in touch with their London office askin' them to try an' find out — that's how we came into it.'

'They commissioned Howard to find out if there was any truth in the rumour that Manners had discovered this uranium,' said Halliday, 'and what had happened to the map showing the locality? Is that right?'

'That's right,' said Chives.

'What made him join this concert party?' asked the Superintendent. 'What had they got to do with it?'

'The pilot of the plane — 'is name was Jim Lester — 'ad a brother who was in the concert party business. Howard thought 'e might know something about what 'ad 'appened to the map. You see, we didn't know whether Jim Lester was straight or not. It all looked a fishy business. All we knew was that Manners had told him about the uranium 'e'd found.'

'You didn't know that this fellow, Lester, had sent the map and photographs to Manners' solicitor, Granger, as he'd been asked?' said Halliday.

Chives shook his head.

'No,' he said. 'We 'ad practically

nothin' to go on at first — only what this nurse 'ad picked up when Lester was delirious. Then we found out that this feller, Beatal, was mixed up in it. I got in with 'im by pretending that I knew somethin' an' was willing to 'elp him if he paid well. That's when we first 'eard about Granger and the other two, Hargreaves an' Renton.'

It was coming straight, thought Halliday. The tangle was slowly unravelling itself. He said:

'What's the name of Jim Lester's brother?'

'D'yer mean 'is real name or 'is stage name?' asked Chives.

'What's the name he's using in this concert party?' asked the Superintendent.

'Billy Dale,' answered Chives.

'Bring him in, Soames,' said Halliday. 'Let's see what Mr. Billy Dale has to say for himself.'

Billy came in. He was not looking very happy and he glanced quickly from one to the other questioningly.

'I've told you all I know,' he said. 'And that's nothing.'

'I don't think you've told us all you know, Mr. Dale,' said Halliday. 'Jim Lester was your brother, wasn't he?'

Billy was obviously taken aback. This was something he had not expected.

'Well, yes, he was,' he admitted.

'Why didn't you tell us that before?'

'Why should I?' demanded Billy in evident surprise. 'What on earth has my brother got to do with it?'

His astonishment appeared quite genuine.

'When did you last hear from him?' asked Halliday.

'Nearly a year ago,' replied Billy, 'and that was only a postcard. Then I heard he'd died from injuries in a plane crash.'

His face clouded.

'You know nothing about the discovery of a uranium deposit in Northern Saskatchewan?' asked the Superintendent.

Billy looked at him as though he'd taken leave of his senses.

'Uranium deposit?' He shook his head. 'What on earth are you talking about?'

'Your brother was piloting a plane for

David Manners when he crashed,' said Halliday watching him keenly. 'Didn't you know that?'

Billy shook his head.

'No,' he answered. 'David Man — ' He stopped suddenly. 'Manners, did you say? That was the name of the girl . . . '

'Exactly,' Halliday's voice was stern. 'You say you knew nothing about David Manners?'

'I didn't,' declared Billy. 'This is the first I've heard about it . . . '

'It seems a very extraordinary thing to me,' said the Superintendent, 'that you knew nothing about all this.'

'Perhaps it does,' retorted Billy. 'But it's the truth, all the same.'

'Who took the packet from Mr. Wayne's dressing room?' asked Halliday suddenly.

'Not me, if that's what you're suggesting,' said Billy.

'He's right about that,' interjected Chives. 'I took it.'

Halliday was surprised.

'You?' he said. 'Did you also take the one from Miss Lee's lodgings?'

'Yes,' said Chives. 'We thought we'd got what we wanted but they were both fakes.'

'Granger was lying, then,' grunted Halliday. 'He's still got the real packet.'

'I don't know anything about this at all,' put in Billy.

'You must realise, Mr. Dale,' said Halliday, 'that you're in a very serious position. Two murders have been committed . . . '

'I say, look here,' exclaimed Billy in dismay. 'You're not trying to pin those on me?'

'I'm only trying to find out the truth,' said Halliday.

'You'd better try some other way,' retorted Billy. 'I didn't even believe them when they said they'd found that girl in the basket . . . '

He stopped as he realised what he'd said.

'What basket?' demanded Halliday sharply.

'Oh, my lord,' stammered Billy. 'Now, I have put my foot in it. I didn't . . . ' His voice trailed away to silence.

'I think,' said Halliday sternly, 'that you'd better go on with what you were going to tell me.'

'Well,' explained the unhappy Billy. 'It was the prop basket . . . I thought they were joking when they said they'd found her in it.'

'Who found her?' asked Halliday.

'Andy McKay and Tony . . . I thought they were pulling my leg. When I looked in the basket there was only a dummy from the waxworks . . . '

'Let me get this straight,' said Halliday rubbing his forehead. 'McKay and Wayne found the body of Thelma Granger in one of those baskets in the passage?'

'That's what they told me,' said Billy. 'Is that who she was? They thought it was the other girl . . . '

'What's all this about a waxworks dummy?' asked Halliday.

'I can tell you about that,' broke in Chives. 'That was Beatal's idea.'

He proceeded to tell them . . .

15

'Well, what do we do now?' demanded Hargreaves when Halliday and Soames had gone hurrying off to the Dome Pavilion with Chives.

Granger shrugged his shoulders.

'There doesn't seem to be much choice, does there?' he said. 'We can't do anything without the map and the photographs and we're not likely to get them now.'

'A nice mess you've made of the whole thing, haven't you,' sneered Renton. He went over and poured himself out a drink. 'The whole thing makes me mad!'

'It's no good blaming me,' said Granger.

'Well, who's fault is it?' snapped Renton. 'If you hadn't tried to be so damned clever . . . '

'What's the good of going all over that again,' broke in Hargreaves impatiently. 'The question is — are we going to try and find the real packet or are we going to give the whole thing up?'

Simon Beatal laughed.

'A very pertinent question, sir,' he said, 'Personally, I would suggest the latter course.'

'Well, there's nothing to stop you,' grunted Renton, gulping down his whisky.

'I'm inclined to agree with Beatal,' said Hargreaves. He rubbed his chin. 'It's getting too dangerous.'

'You're a lot of white-livered curs!' snarled Kenton.

'It's no use talking like that,' said Hargreaves. 'We've got to be careful. We're in a very nasty position.'

'Exactly, sir,' agreed Simon Beatal. 'The police are now in possession of the facts. Even if we obtained the real packet now it is doubtful if we could use it to any useful purpose.'

'We could register the claim,' said Renton.

'On behalf of Miss Manners, sir?' Beatal shook his head. 'What good would that do us? The cat is out of the bag, sir. Before it was known that David Manners had discovered this uranium location it was a proposition — an extremely good proposition. Now . . . He shrugged his enormous shoulders and shook his head.

'I see,' said Renton and there was a dangerous look on his face. 'So we just pack up and let whoever stole that packet reap the benefit.'

'Not at all, sir,' said Simon Beatal. 'There will be no benefit to reap — unless it is conferred by the public hangman. There have been two murders, sir — Mrs. Granger and this detective posing as a concert party artist . . . '

'That's got nothing to do with us,' said Renton.

'In the eyes of the police, sir, it has a great deal to do with us,' said Beatal. 'I assure you, sir, that with the exception of Miss Manners, anyone attempting to register that claim would find themselves in an extremely awkward position. My advice to you, gentlemen, is — cut your losses.'

Renton laughed contemptuously.

'You're easily scared, aren't you?' he sneered.

'I am not a fool, sir,' retorted the fat man. 'There are times when discretion is the better part of valour — to use a well-known cliché. In my opinion this is one of them.'

'He's right, you know,' said Hargreaves.

'I'm glad, sir,' said Simon Beatal, 'that you agree with me. We have failed in our little — shall we say business enterprise? It is the act of a wise man, sir, to turn to something fresh.' He rose ponderously to his feet, picked up his hat and gloves, and went over to the door. 'I wish you all a very good day,' he said and went out. They heard his jerky laugh until the front door shut behind him.

'Well, I must say he's a pretty good loser,' said Hargreaves.

Renton looked at him and shook his head.

'I wish I knew what his game is,' he said.

'What do you mean?' asked Granger.

'You don't really believe he means to quit, do you?' asked Renton. He gave a harsh laugh. 'You're so simple you wouldn't know when to come in out of the rain.'

'He can't do anything,' said Hargreaves with conviction. 'As he said the thing's become too dangerous. He's sensible enough to know that.'

'I'd soon do something if I had that packet,' said Renton.

'You talk a lot,' said Granger. 'I'd like to know just what you could do.'

'Legally it belongs to this girl — Jill Manners, doesn't it?' said Renton.

'Yes, and the police know it,' said Hargreaves. 'That's the whole trouble.'

'The police, the police!' mocked Renton. 'What are you — a lot of frightened kids?'

Granger made a gesture of irritation,

'It's no good being stupid about it, Renton,' he said. 'We're just as much upset over the thing as you are. But the plain truth is we none of us stand an earthly chance of claiming that uranium. Not now.'

'It was totally different before,' said Hargreaves, 'when nobody knew that Manners had left it to his daughter.'

'What difference does that make?' demanded Renton.

Hargreaves stared at him.

'You're mad!' he snapped.

'Am I?' retorted Renton. 'I'm saner than the rest of you. I don't intend to give up a fortune just because someone gets up and says 'boo'.'

'All right, all right,' said Granger. 'Let's hear what you propose to do about it? Tell us about this wonderful plan you've got.'

'You tell me something first,' said Renton. 'Suppose that girl made a will leaving everything to you. What happens then?'

Granger laughed.

'Nothing. Not while she ... ' He stopped abruptly.

'Not while she's alive. That's what you were going to say, isn't it?'

'I know what's in your mind,' Hargreaves interrupted quickly. 'I'll have no part in it.'

'Oh, do stop talking like the village preacher,' cried Renton angrily. 'I've never come across such a lot of mealy-mouthed ... '

'I've no wish to swing at the end of a rope,' snapped Hargreaves. 'You can

209

please yourself, but I'm having nothing to do with it.'

'We'd never get away with it, Renton,' said Granger. 'We'd be suspected at once. A child could see that.'

'Not,' said Renton slowly, 'if it was an accident . . . '

He looked from one to the other of them meaningfully.

'Do you think the police would swallow that, you fool, after what's happened?' Granger uttered a short laugh that was like a bark. 'They'd be on to it in a second. They're not idiots.'

'So long as they couldn't prove anything,' said Renton coolly, 'it wouldn't matter what they suspected, would it?'

Granger frowned. He walked over to the window and stared out into the garden. After a moment he turned.

'It's far too risky,' he said, shaking his head. 'Besides, we'd never get Jill to make a will . . . '

'You don't have to tell her what it is, do you?' demanded Renton. 'Surely you're smart enough to get her to sign something without her knowing what she's signing? You can fill in all the rest — after you've got her signature . . . '

'You're not seriously considering this suggestion of Renton's, are you, Granger?' said Hargreaves. 'You must be mad.'

'You shut up,' said Renton. 'I'm doing the talking now.'

'I'll have no part in it, I tell you,' said Hargreaves.

'Very well, stay out then,' snarled Renton. 'There'll be all the more for me and Granger.'

'You're welcome to the lot, my friend, if you can get it,' said Granger with an unpleasant smile. 'I'm not having any-thing to do with it either.'

An ugly expression came into Renton's face.

'You've got no guts, either of you,' he cried disgustedly.

'You've plenty — that's what you appear to be thinking with,' retorted Granger. 'Have some sense, Renton. If there was any safe and workable scheme by which we could get hold of this fortune, I'd be only too pleased to find it. But there isn't . . . '

'I've shown you how we can still cash in on this business,' said Renton obstinately.

'You've only shown us how we'd end up on the gallows,' said Hargreaves. 'Forget it.'

'There must be a way,' said Renton. 'There must. Why don't you try and think up something? I'll bet Beatal does.'

'Beatal's given it up,' said Granger.

Renton laughed.

'If you believe that you'll believe anything,' he said derisively. 'He's got some scheme up his sleeve, don't you kid yourselves.'

'Beatal's helpless. There's nothing he can do,' declared Hargreaves confidently.

But there he underestimated Simon Beatal's cunning.

★ ★ ★

The little group in the stage door passage at the Dome Pavilion were growing a trifle restive. The time was getting on and they had received no intimation from Superintendent Halliday that they could go.

Billy Dale had been in the dressing room where Halliday was holding the investigation for what seemed hours, a fact that made them uneasy.

'Billy's in there a long time, isn't he?' muttered Vera. She was looking anxious and strained.

'I wonder why they sent for him?' said Beryl.

'I expect they want to question each of us in turn,' said Andy.

'But they've already done that,' said Vera. 'Why do we have to go through it all again?'

'They've their own methods, I've no doubt,' said Andy. 'It's no good getting upset. Ye'll just have to grin and bear it.'

'It'll be time for the matinée soon,' grumbled Vera. 'And we've had nothing to eat.'

'Ye'll just have to make do with a sandwich,' said Andy.

'I always thought there was something queer about that man, Gilbert,' she snapped viciously, 'and now look what he's let us in for?'

'Aye, I've no doubt he got himself

strangled just to spite us,' said Andy.

The stage door opened and Sharon came in quickly. Her face showed that she had heard what had happened.

'I say,' she greeted them, 'isn't this shocking — about Howard Gilbert. The policeman's just told me outside. He wouldn't let me come in until I told him I was one of the concert party. What's happening now?'

'The police think one of us did it,' said Vera.

Sharon looked at her in horrified astonishment.

'Oh, no!' she exclaimed.

'They're questioning Billy now,' said Beryl.

'Billy — what does he know about it?'

'No more than the rest of us,' said Tony. 'Its just a matter of routine, I think.'

She ignored him, deliberately turning her back.

'What are you going to do about Gilbert's numbers?' she asked Andy. He shrugged his shoulders

'We'll have to rearrange the programme,' he said. 'You can do an extra number and I'll put in the comedy trio with Tony and Vera we were rehearsing this morning.'

'I can't understand all this,' said Sharon wrinkling her forehead. 'Why should anyone want to kill Gilbert?'

'His name wasn't Gilbert. It was John Howard,' said Vera. 'He was a detective.'

Sharon's eyes opened wide.

'A detective,' she exclaimed. 'What was he doing here?'

Before anyone could answer her, the door of Gilbert's dressing room opened and Billy came out. He was looking a little strained and wan.

'Will you go in, Andy?' he said.

Andy nodded and went in. The door closed behind him Billy wiped his face with his handkerchief.

'Phew!' he said thankfully, 'I'm glad that's over. They want to see you, Tony, after Andy, but the rest of us can go.'

'Thank heaven for that,' said Vera. 'Who's coming for something to eat?'

'I'll wait for Andy,' said Beryl.

Sharon, Vera and Billy went off together leaving Tony and Beryl alone.

'Beryl,' said Tony rather hesitantly, 'I — I wish you'd do me a favour.'

'Of course, dear,' she said, 'if I can. What is it?'

'It's about Sharon . . . '

'Sharon?'

'She's — she's got the needle . . . '

'With you?'

Tony nodded.

'Yes . . . ' He found it difficult to put it into words. 'You see, I'd promised to meet her for tea the other afternoon and — and I didn't. I took Vera instead . . . '

'Well, I'm not surprised Sharon was cross,' said Beryl. 'I should have been livid.'

'You don't understand,' explained Tony hastily. 'I didn't do it on purpose . . . At least, not for the reason Sharon thinks. I wanted to find out something from Vera. It was to do with the packet . . . '

'Well, why don't you explain to her?' said Beryl.

'She won't let me,' said Tony. 'She's gone all upstage . . . I thought perhaps . . . if you would . . . '

'Do a little interceding for you?' She

helped him out as he floundered badly.

'Yes, she won't freeze *you* up,' he said.

'I'll do my best, dear,' said Beryl kindly.

'Thanks,' he said fervently. 'You're a good sort, Beryl.'

She sighed a little sadly.

'I wish you'd tell Andy that,' she said.

Andy was a long time with Halliday but he reappeared at last and intimated that Tony was to go in.

'He's a wee bit riled that we didna tell him about finding her in the basket,' he whispered.

'How did he know about it?' asked Tony.

'Billy,' said Andy. 'Go on, go and get it over.'

'Andy,' said Beryl as Tony left them, 'let's go and have some coffee.'

Andy was so shaken that morning that he scarcely knew what he was saying.

'Aye, I could do with a cup,' he said to Beryl's amazed delight.

She seized him by the arm before he could change his mind and whisked him out of the stage door.

'I'll just pop into the box office first,' he

said as they came round the front of the Dome but Beryl tightened her grip on his arm.

'You'll do nothing of the kind,' she said grimly. 'You'll have the coffee first.'

And Andy meekly obeyed.

* * *

Superintendent Halliday came into his office and sank into his chair behind the desk. He had had very little sleep on the previous night and it was now late in the afternoon. There was a report on his desk and he glanced at it idly.

'Well, Soames,' he said to the Sergeant who had followed him in, 'we've got two murders now instead of one, and we're no nearer putting our hand on the murderer than we were before.'

'We know a good deal more about it though, sir,' said Soames.

'Maybe we do,' agreed Halliday rubbing his forehead, 'but it doesn't tell us who out of this bunch is the strangler.'

'It must have been one of the concert party people, sir,' said the Sergeant.

218

'Which one?'

'Well, sir, I'd say it was Dale.'

'He seems the most likely but there isn't any evidence.'

'He was the original reason Howard joined the concert party, sir,' said Soames.

'He was trying to find a lead — anything that would put him on to this uranium business,' said Halliday. 'He knew that Dale was Jim Lester's brother so he tried that. There's nothing to show that he discovered anything against him. On the contrary, according to Chives, as soon as he learned about Beatal and Granger he transferred his attention to them.'

'He might have found something out that made him switch it back again to Dale, sir.'

'He might equally well have found something that switched it to someone else,' said Halliday a trifle irritably. 'It's all 'might'. There's nothing solid. There's only one thing we can be certain of — that this uranium discovery of David Manners is at the bottom of everything.'

'Chives knew all about that, sir,' said Soames.

'Chives!' Halliday looked up at him sharply.

'What are you getting at, Soames?'

'I was just wondering, sir,' said the Sergeant, 'if perhaps Chives might know a lot more than he's said.'

'It's an idea, Soames,' said Halliday. He lay back in his chair frowning and tapping his fingers nervously on the desk. 'Chives? Um. We've only his word that those packets were dummies. The one he stole from Vera Lee's lodgings might have been the real thing.'

'And then he would have had to get rid of Howard, sir, if he'd wanted to keep it for himself,' said Soames.

'By jove, you may be on to something,' said Halliday. 'I must say I never thought of Chives but, of course, when you come to look at it, he stands out. He knew all about the whole thing from the beginning. If he'd decided to grab the uranium for himself . . . Um, maybe Granger was speaking the truth when he swore that the packet he'd given to the Lee girl was genuine . . . I wish we could do something about that bunch, Soames, but the trouble is we can't. Except Beatal. We could have him for moving that woman's body but what good would that do? It'd only be a minor charge and we're after bigger fish.'

'Chives helped him move the woman, sir,' said the Sergeant.

'Chives again, eh?' Halliday frowned thoughtfully. 'Howard was knocked unconscious before he was strangled,' he touched the report on his desk. 'This is the doctor's report. That would make it easier, you see.'

'Howard was sitting down when he was killed,' said Soames. 'He must've been taken by surprise or he'd have got up . . . '

'Meaning he didn't suspect the person who came in,' said Halliday.

'Yes, sir,' said Soames.

They looked at each other.

'He wouldn't have suspected Chives,' said Halliday. 'Yes — I think we must pay more attention to Chives — but there's no evidence, you know, no evidence at all . . . '

16

Andy came into the dressing room to change after the matinée and his face was worried.

'What's the matter, Andy?' asked Tony. 'Bad house? It looked pretty good to me.'

'Aye, there was nothing the matter with the house,' said Andy. 'It's the show. It's going to pieces. Vera dried up in the middle of her number and Billy started playing the wrong introduction for Sharon. If it had no been for Beryl keeping her head there'd have been a terrible mix-up. I don't know what's the matter with everybody.'

'It's not difficult to guess, is it?' asked Tony.

'Ye mean all this trouble?' asked Andy. Tony nodded.

'Yes,' he said. 'It's nerves, that's all . . . '

'They shouldna let it affect the show,' said Andy.

'You're a bit dithery yourself,' said Tony

eyeing him critically. 'Now, admit it?'

'Aye, I am. But I don't let it interfere with my work.'

'Have you heard anything more from Halliday?'

'No, and I dinna want to,' said Andy. 'I'm fed up with all of it. I've got to get someone down from London to take Gilbert's place and that'll mean more rehearsals and a whole lot of work just when things were beginning to settle down nicely.'

Billy came in quickly.

'I say, Andy,' he said apologetically. 'I'm terribly sorry about this afternoon . . . '

'Aye, what happened to ye?' said Andy. 'You ought to know what Sharon's singing by now . . . '

'I know, I've got absolutely no excuse at all,' said Billy contritely. 'It's just that all this business is getting me down.'

'It's getting us all down,' said Tony. 'Why did you have to tell Halliday about the girl in the basket?'

'I'm sorry about that,' said Billy. 'I couldn't help it. It just slipped out before I'd realised what I'd said.'

He began rapidly to take off his make-up.

'I wonder what the police really think,' he said.

'Aye, I'd like to know that myself,' said Andy. 'If only that wretched girl hadn't thrown that packet into our compartment.'

'Yes, that's what started the trouble,' agreed Billy.

'Did it?' said Tony. 'I wonder. Gilbert or Howard was here before that wasn't he?'

'He was here because of me,' said Billy. They stared at him.

'Because of you?' said Andy. 'What do you mean?'

Billy explained and they listened with interest.

'I knew nothing about the packet or what it contained or anything about the wretched business, but, of course, it looked bad to Halliday,' he ended.

'So that's the secret of the packet, is it?' said Andy. 'Uranium, eh?'

Tony whistled.

'No wonder all these people were so

anxious to get it,' he exclaimed. 'Why, the value must be fabulous . . . '

'And it all belongs to the red-haired girl on the train,' said Billy. 'You know,' he added with a touch of his old humour, 'I knew I ought to have got acquainted with her. Something told me she was the girl I've always been looking for. Slim, beautiful, attractive — and with oodles of uranium thrown in. I could settle up with a girl like that and my creditors would live happily ever after.'

'In the meanwhile,' said Andy practically, 'ye'd better pay attention to your job. Ye know, I'm more than a wee bit worried.'

'I'll be all right, Andy,' said Billy. 'I won't make any more bloomers in the show.'

'It wasna the show I was thinking of then,' said Andy seriously. 'I was thinking about this business of that poor girl and Gilbert.'

'What were you thinking?' asked Tony.

'Somebody killed them,' said Andy. 'I'm thinking I'll be happier when we know who it was.'

He didn't explain why but Tony guessed.

Andy was afraid that it might turn out to be someone they knew. Someone in the concert party.

'You know,' said Billy, washing his hands in the basin, 'I've always been hoping for some sort of excitement like you read about in books. Do you know the kind I mean? Some glamorous female, all willowy and seductive, sidles up to you, breathing a rare perfume, and whispers: 'Tonight at twelve. The postern gate. Black Domino'. Something of that sort. The nearest I ever got to it was my landlady's daughter at Wigan and she'd been eating onions.'

Tony laughed.

'What happened?' he asked.

'She said: 'There's a smashing film at the Orpheum. What about it, ducks'?' Billy shook his head sadly. 'I didn't go,' he said. 'There is nothing seductive and mysterious about onions!'

There was a tap on the dressing room door and Vera's voice called: 'Are you ready, Billy?'

'Just coming, darling,' answered Billy, slipping on his jacket.

'Hurry up,' she said. 'I'll wait outside on the pier.'

'All right,' shouted Billy. 'I shan't be a tick.'

He brushed his hair quickly.

'Vera's the nearest you'll get to your seductive female,' said Tony. 'You'll have to put up with her.'

Billy went over to the door.

'I might do worse,' he said and went out.

Andy frowned at his own reflection in the mirror.

'It's a funny thing, isn't it?' he said.

'What?' asked Tony.

'Those two being so friendly.'

'Vera's crazy about Billy,' said Tony. 'She always has been — ever since she joined the company.'

'Aye, I know.' Andy nodded. 'His brother was the pilot of that plane and Vera brought the packet . . .'

'Good lord,' exclaimed Tony, 'you're not suggesting that . . .'

'I'm no' suggesting anything,' said Andy

quickly. 'But I don't like it — I don't like it at all . . . '

★　★　★

Everybody had gone when Tony finally left the Dome Pavilion. It was very hot and oppressive, a thick heavy heat, that made his head feel as though it was full of cotton wool. Away out to sea, along the horizon, a bank of cloud was gathering, dark solid looking cloud with livid edges, that foreshadowed a storm.

The sea was smooth, rolling gently in to the beach with a sluggishness that had a suggestion of oil.

Tony felt worried and depressed.

Andy had succeeded in passing on his own uneasiness. That, and the attitude that Sharon had adopted, filled him with an acute sense of utter dejection.

He walked along the front until he found a small café that was not overcrowded and had some tea. It was a good pot of tea. Not like the dishwater that he and Vera had been given that afternoon when she had told him about the man who had given her the packet to bring down. If he had never bothered about that, if he had kept his nose out of the whole business, there would never have been this trouble with Sharon . . .

Coming out of the café he came face to face with Simon Beatal.

'We seem destined to meet again, sir,' said the fat man. 'A lovely afternoon but there are storm clouds blowing up.' He laughed. 'Yes, sir, there are definitely storm clouds on the horizon.' His heavy jowls shook as he laughed again and Tony noticed the tiny mole at the corner of his small mouth.

'I am glad, sir, to have this opportunity of wishing you goodbye,' continued Simon Beatal. 'I am leaving tomorrow morning, sir, and I doubt if our paths will cross in the future.'

'So you've given up trying to do Miss Manners out of her property?' said Tony.

'A crude way of putting it, sir,' said the fat man, 'but fundamentally correct. As a business man, sir, I cannot afford to waste time on a project that is no longer likely to reach fruition.'

'I'm very glad to hear it,' said Tony. 'I suppose your friends, Hargreaves, Renton and Granger have given it up too, eh?'

'No friends of mine, I assure you, sir,' said Simon Beatal. 'I may have considered at one period of associating with them in a purely business capacity but we have nothing in common.'

'Except that you're all consummate scoundrels,' retorted Tony.

'There are, sir,' said Simon Beatal, 'different degrees in these matters. I regret to have to say that the persons you mention are of the lowest. Crude, sir, crude.' He laughed. 'Well, sir, I wish you a very good day and prosperity for the future. I regret that it is unlikely that we shall meet again, sir.'

'I'm sorry I can't reciprocate your regrets,' said Tony.

'You are unkind, sir, you are unkind,' said Simon Beatal shaking his head. 'However, I bear you no malice. Goodbye, sir.'

He moved away along the front and Tony watched his huge immaculately clad figure towering above the crowd of holidaymakers until it became lost to view.

There was an hour and a half before he need return to the Dome Pavilion for the evening show and he decided to go for a walk. He took the path that led up to the cliff top. It was quieter here and less crowded.

Something was niggling at the back of his mind but he couldn't discover what it was. Something to do with Simon Beatal? It might have been but he wasn't sure.

Walking slowly along, he began to go over in his mind all that had happened since the girl in black had thrown that packet into the compartment of the train. He forced himself to do this in order to keep himself from thinking about Sharon. The arrival of the girl to claim the packet . . . the horrible moment when they had discovered the body in the basket . . . Vera's connection with the other packet . . . Billy . . . the second visit of Jill Manners, interrupted by the arrival of Simon Beatal . . .

And suddenly he stopped dead in his walk.

Standing perfectly still, he stared quite unseeingly out to the now dark and heavy clouds that were massing on the horizon.

The thing that had been worrying at his mind had suddenly become crystal clear — like something picked out with a searchlight.

He couldn't be mistaken, and if he wasn't mistaken . . .

He turned abruptly and began to walk rapidly back the way he had come. Half-way along the front he turned off into the town and presently came to the police station. Entering, he inquired of the sergeant in charge for Superintendent Halliday.

'He's not in, sir,' said the man. 'He'll be back presently. Is there anything I can do?'

Tony thought for a moment and then shook his head.

'No,' he replied, 'I must see Superintendent Halliday.'

'I can give him a message when he comes in,' said the Sergeant.

'Tell him Anthony Wayne called,' said Tony. 'Ask him if he can get in touch with me at the Dome Pavilion this evening. Tell him it's urgent.'

The Sergeant looked at him curiously.

'Very good, sir,' he said. 'I'll tell the Superintendent.'

Tony left the police station and made his way to the pier.

He wanted the seclusion of his dressing room to quietly consider the startling discovery he had made. Not that he had the slightest doubt that he was right but to work out in detail just what that discovery meant.

And by the time Andy came in to make-up for the evening show, he was certain that he had found the murderer.

17

The storm burst over Westpool just before ten. The rain came down in torrents and the wind lashed the sea to fury so that it smashed angrily against the rocks and broke in huge waves over the drenched promenade. The thunder and lightning were incessant, pealing and flickering over the boiling sea with the effect of an inferno. It drove the crowds of holiday-makers to seek shelter so that the front and the town were soon deserted and Westpool, that a few hours before had been so gay and noisy, was like a city of the dead.

'My lord, what a night,' said Tony as he came off the stage and met Andy in the passage. 'The thunder almost drowned Vera's number, and the rain on the roof sounds like a hundred drums.'

'Aye,' said Andy, 'but it's a wonderful house. They're packed in like sardines.'

He hurried up on to the stage and Tony

went on to his dressing room. As he nearly reached it, Sharon came out of hers. She would have passed him without speaking but he stopped her.

'I say,' he said, 'don't go on like this . . . '

'I'm not going on like anything,' she said. 'Please let me pass.'

'Didn't Beryl talk to you?' he asked.

'She frequently talks to me,' retorted Sharon. 'I'm in a hurry.'

'I mean about me,' said Tony.

She looked at him coldly.

'I believe she did try to tell me something,' she said, 'I wasn't interested.'

She hurried away, leaving Tony staring after her.

The stage door opened at that moment and he turned quickly to see Superintendent Halliday come in.

'I've just got your message, sir,' said Halliday. 'You said the matter was urgent so, in spite of the storm, I thought I'd better come along at once.'

He shook the water from his shiny oilskin.

'I'm glad you did,' said Tony. 'Come in

here. We shan't be disturbed for a few minutes.'

He ushered the Superintendent into his dressing room and shut the door.

'Now, sir,' said Halliday. 'What's this all about?'

Tony told him as briefly and quickly as possible.

Halliday listened attentively and the expression on his face changed to one of incredulity and amazement.

'You're quite sure about this, sir?' he asked when Tony had finished. 'You couldn't have been mistaken?'

Tony shook his head emphatically.

'No,' he said. 'It wasn't there . . .'

★   ★   ★

Up on the top of North Cliff the wind reached gale force. It blew in from the sea in great tempestuous gusts that howled mournfully round the caravan that had belonged to David Manners. It shook the door and rattled the windows, driving before it the rain so that it beat a continuous tattoo on the glass.

Inside the small living room, the red-haired girl was moving restlessly about smoking a cigarette. There was a frown on her face and she flinched as each successive peal of thunder went rolling and echoing overhead. Presently she stubbed out her cigarette in an ashtray and went into the small kitchen. She made herself some coffee on the Calor gas stove and, carrying it back into the sitting room, sat down near a small table. The frown on her face deepened as she sipped the coffee. After a moment or two she looked at the watch on her wrist. It was nearly half past ten.

A clap of thunder, louder than any of the preceding ones, seemed to shake the earth, and the blue-white glare of lightning lit up the dark squares of the small windows.

The girl shivered and, getting up, drew the curtains.

She had scarcely reseated herself and picked up the remains of her coffee, when there came a tap at the door. She had heard no sound of an approaching car or footsteps but the noise of the storm would have drowned any sounds.

'Who is it?' she called nervously.

'It's me,' answered a man's voice. 'Open the door.'

She went over to the door and unlocked it.

Granger came in hastily. His raincoat and hat were streaming with water and he took off his hat and shook it.

'What a night,' he grunted, flinging his hat on a chair.

'Why did you come?' she asked. 'What do you want?'

She moved away from the door forgetting to relock it.

'I had to talk to you,' he said.

'Why?' she looked at him anxiously. 'Everything's all right, isn't it?'

The handle of the door turned softly and it opened an inch but they were unaware of the fact.

'Yes, yes,' said Granger, 'there's nothing to worry about. It's all plain sailing now. Tomorrow you can go back to London — turn up at the office and wait for me. I'll get back as soon as I can. After a few weeks I'll register the claim . . . '

'In whose name, sir?' inquired a voice behind them.

They swung round. Simon Beatal stood in the open doorway. A gust of wind came whistling in and blew round the cosy interior of the caravan. The fat man closed the door.

'What the devil are you doing here?' exclaimed Granger.

'I followed you, sir,' replied Simon Beatal. 'An unpleasant task on such a night — but, I hope, rewarding.'

'What do you want?' demanded Granger.

'An answer to my question first, sir,' said the fat man smiling blandly. 'In whose name are you registering the claim?'

'Jill Manners, of course,' snapped Granger. 'It's no good you thinking you're going to get a cut in it because you won't. It belongs rightfully to Jill and Jill's going to have it.'

Simon Beatal laughed.

'Indeed, sir,' he said. 'I was not aware that it was possible to register a claim in the name of a deceased person, sir.'

'I don't know what you're talking about, Beatal,' snapped Granger angrily. 'If this is some more of your . . . '

'Come, come, sir,' interrupted Simon Beatal, still smiling. 'You may be able to deceive people like Hargreaves and Renton — even Superintendent Halliday — but I, sir, am a different proposition, I assure you. I am not so easily hoodwinked, sir.'

The red-haired girl looked at him with frightened eyes and then turned to Granger.

'What does he mean?' she asked.

'I don't know,' retorted Granger. 'He's up to some jiggery-pokery . . . '

'You wish me to explain, sir?' said Simon Beatal.

'If you can,' snapped Granger. 'And you'd better be quick about it. I want to get back.'

'Very well, sir,' said the fat man. 'It is quite obvious to me that it was Jill Manners who was killed. This lady is her sister, sir, Thelma Granger — your wife.'

He bowed to the girl.

'You're mad!' cried Granger.

'Let us ask Mrs. Granger if she agrees with you, sir,' said Beatal. 'She is in a better position to know than either of us, since it was she who killed her sister.'

'Oh, no . . . you're wrong. I didn't. Why should I want to kill Thelma?'

'Not Thelma,' said the fat man. 'Jill. You are Thelma.'

She stared at him in amazement.

'It isn't true,' she said. 'It isn't true . . . '

'Of course, it isn't true,' broke in Granger. 'What's the idea, Beatal? If you think you can get away with these accusations . . . '

'Come now, my dear Mrs. Granger,' said Simon Beatal. 'The difference between you and your sister is slight but sufficient for an observant man. I flatter myself that I am very observant. The tiny mole at the corner of your left eye — you see, sir? Jill had no such mole.' He laughed. 'A small thing, sir, but conclusive.'

'I never heard such a lot of utter nonsense,' exclaimed Granger impatiently. 'If you think you're going to get anything by all this rubbish, Beatal . . . '

'That is why I am here, sir,' replied Simon Beatal smoothly. 'I am a business man. I am willing to overlook the regrettable fact that your wife killed her sister and was also responsible for the death of that unfortunate private detective . . . '

'I didn't . . . I didn't do anything . . . ' cried the girl with tears in her eyes. 'Oh, please, Mr. Granger . . . You know it isn't true.'

'Of course I know it isn't true, Jill,' said Granger. 'You're making all this up, Beatal, to try and extort money out of Miss Manners. Well, it isn't going to work . . . '

'I must congratulate you, sir,' said Simon Beatal. 'You do it exceedingly well. An admirable performance, sir. Both you and your wife would be an asset to the stage, sir. But it doesn't convince me.'

'That's too bad,' sneered Granger.

'I am not at all sure, sir, that it would convince Superintendent Halliday,' remarked Simon Beatal. 'However, it will prove of great interest to see. I will wish you good night, Mrs. Granger. Good night, sir.'

He bowed and turned to the door.

'Wait!' said Granger harshly.

The fat man turned back.

'You wish me to stay, sir?' he asked blandly.

'You've no proof, you know — not an atom,' said Granger.

'A full investigation by the police would, I venture to believe, provide all the proof necessary,' replied Simon Beatal. 'A mere hint is all that is required, sir, to start such an investigation.'

There was a crash of thunder and the caravan shook.

'What do you want?' demanded Granger bluntly.

'Now, you are being wise, sir,' said Simon Beatal. He laughed. 'Shall we settle for a half-share?'

'No!' snapped Granger. 'We'll settle for nothing!'

He fired the shot through his pocket. The huge figure of Simon Beatal sagged and crumpled slowly. For a moment it swayed and then it fell with a thud to the floor. It twitched convulsively and then lay still.

'You fool!' cried the girl.

Granger drew the automatic from his pocket and rubbed his thumb where the blow-back had made a reddish burn.

'It was the only thing to do,' he muttered.

'Supposing someone heard the shot?' she demanded. 'What then?'

'In this storm?' He shook his head. 'You couldn't hear anything a yard away.'

She stared down at the ungainly body and her forehead puckered.

'What are we going to do with him?' she muttered.

'It's not very far to the edge of the cliff,' he said. 'I could get him there, I think.'

'I don't like it,' she said. 'They'll find the body and they'll know he was shot. It won't take very long to connect him with you . . . '

'They can't prove anything,' he said.

'Can't they? You were a fool to have done it.'

'It's a bit late in the day for you to start getting squeamish, Thelma,' he said. 'There was nothing else to be done. We should have had him tacked on to us for the rest of our lives. Do you think he'd have been satisfied with a half-share? He'd have had the lot before he was through.'

'I suppose you're right,' she agreed. She went over to the table and took a cigarette from a packet and lit it. Blowing out a cloud of smoke she sat down and cupped her chin in her hand.

'Listen,' she said after a pause, 'can't we fix this on Hargreaves or Renton?'

'How?' he asked quickly.

'See what he's got in his pockets,' she said coolly.

He went over to the body and made a rapid search.

'There's nothing very much here,' he said presently, straightening up. 'A wallet, a small notebook, a fountain pen . . . '

'The wallet and the notebook will do,' she said quickly. 'You're going back to Hargreaves' bungalow, aren't you?'

He nodded.

'When you get back plant the wallet and the notebook somewhere — in Hargreaves' wardrobe perhaps — and put the pistol with them . . . '

He looked admiringly.

'Thelma,' he exclaimed, 'that's damned clever . . . '

'I always had to think for you,' she said

a little contemptuously. 'You'd never have done anything about this uranium business on your own.'

She looked at the sprawling, mountainous body of Simon Beatal.

'Now,' she said, 'you'd better get rid of that.'

There was another terrific crash of thunder and behind the drawn curtains a white glare flickered.

'There shouldn't be anyone about tonight,' he said. 'At the best of times it's pretty lonely up here.'

He stooped, put his hands under Simon Beatal's shoulders and tried to lift him. But he couldn't. He succeeded in raising the body a few inches but that was all. Again he tried, straining every muscle but with the same result.

'I don't think I can do it,' he panted. 'He weighs a ton.'

She frowned.

'We've got to get him out of here somehow,' she said. 'Did you come by car?'

'Yes,' he answered.

'How far did you leave it?'

'On the road . . . '

'Go and get it,' she ordered. 'Drive it as near to the door as you can. There's a grass track — you'll be able to get quite close.'

When he had gone, she went to the cupboard and took out a raincoat. This she put on, switched out the lights, and looked out of the door. It was still pouring with rain and the wind was strong. The lightning blazed and in its revealing whiteness, she could see that the entire cliff top was as deserted as the Sahara desert. There were no houses in the vicinity and it was very doubtful if they would be seen. She was satisfied.

She saw the car come bumping and lurching across the rough grass towards the caravan and presently it stopped within a yard or two of the door.

Granger got out and came towards her.

'What did you do with the real packet?' she asked. 'Did you leave it in London?'

'Trust me,' he said.

'In the office?'

'Yes, in the safe,' he answered. 'It's locked inside a hollowed-out ledger, together with David Manners' last letter. Nobody would ever think there was anything there. It's as safe as houses.'

'Well, let's get this over,' she said.

It was all they could do between them to get the body of Simon Beatal the short distance to the car, but they managed it although it left them both exhausted and breathless.

Granger got in behind the wheel and Thelma slipped into the seat beside him. He started the engine and drove gently towards the cliff edge.

It was not very far and he brought the car to a stop within three yards of the sheer drop to the rocks below.

The rain beat in their faces and the wind tugged at their clothes as they got out and proceeded to haul the heavy body from the back seat.

Another blaze of lightning lit up the cliff top so that it was as bright as day. Granger shot a quick glance round. There was nobody within sight.

'Come on, quickly,' he muttered. 'I shall be glad when this is over.'

Thelma said nothing. With difficulty

they got the body to the cliff edge. One sharp push and all that remained of Simon Beatal went hurtling to the rocks below.

Granger straightened up.

'Now,' he began and it was the last word he ever uttered. Thelma gave him a sudden violent shove and he staggered backwards. For a second he swayed on the extreme edge and then he toppled over and was gone. The scream he gave was drowned in a crash of thunder.

Thelma, her lips set, went quickly to the car. It was pointing towards the cliff edge and she started the engine and put it in gear. It moved forward as she sprang quickly out and its momentum carried it on and over.

She waited only to make sure that it had vanished and then she hurried back through the blinding rain to the caravan. She went in and locked the door, took off her wet raincoat, and switched on the light.

For the next few minutes she was busy tidying the place up. There was no sign of any blood on the floor. Some splashes of water, that was all, nothing to show that anyone except herself had ever been there. Her husband had got the wallet and notebook in his pocket and pistol with which he had shot Beatal. When the bodies were found at the foot of the cliff, they would conclude that there had been a quarrel. The smashed car would be found too — Granger's car. They would wonder what exactly had happened but there was nothing to connect her with any of it. She could go back to London, turn up at the office, still in her role of Jill Manners. The map and the photographs would eventually be found and her father's last letter. Thelma was ostensibly dead. As next of kin she, Jill Manners, would inherit a vast fortune.

She smiled to herself.

It had all worked out as she had planned. All she had to do now was to get away from the caravan at once. No one would know that she had been there that night and she would avoid any awkward questions.

She started to get ready. It was eleven o'clock. There was a train to London at eleven-forty if she could make it.

Hurriedly she packed an overnight bag — a small affair with a zip fastener that was easily carried. She had no wish to attract undue attention to herself by having to enlist the aid of a porter at the station.

She had just finished and was taking a last look round the caravan to make sure that she had forgotten nothing when there came a sharp, authoritative knock on the door.

She turned quickly, her face white under the makeup.

Who was it? Who could it be at this hour?

The knock came again, louder and more impatient A voice that she knew called loudly above the noise of the storm: 'Open up there, please, we wish to see you.'

Superintendent Halliday!

She would *have* to open the door. They knew she must be there. They must have seen the light . . .

She thrust the overnight case under the divan and stripped off her raincoat. After all they couldn't suspect anything . . .

She unlocked the door and opened it.

'What is it?' she asked in a timid voice.

Halliday came in followed by Soames.

'We have a police car outside,' he said without preliminary. 'I must ask you to accompany us to the station for questioning in connection with the murder of ex-Detective Inspector John Howard.'

'Must I come tonight?' she said. 'It's very late . . . '

'I'm sorry, but I'm afraid you must,' said Halliday sternly.

'But — but I don't know anything about it,' she said.

'You will be given an opportunity to prove that, Mrs. Granger,' he retorted. 'In the meanwhile I must warn you that anything you say will be taken down in writing and may be used in evidence hereafter . . . '

She felt as if a cold hand had gripped her heart.

They knew — but they couldn't know . . .

'You're making a mistake,' she said. 'I'm not Mrs. Granger. She was my sister . . . '

'I don't think there's any mistake,' said Halliday.

18

The storm blew itself out during the night and the morning dawned hot and sunny. The promenade and beaches at Westpool became once more thronged with holidaymakers and the pier was crowded. Few of them were aware of the drama that had taken place in their midst or of the patient men who had been working since dawn to recover the bodies of Harold Granger and Simon Beatal and to salvage what remained of the wrecked car.

Lights had burned in the office of Superintendent Halliday far into the night as that weary man pieced together the evidence against Thelma Granger and eventually broke her down.

The news of her arrest reached the members of the concert party when they arrived for the matinée, although it was no news to Tony. It was the memory of that mole on her cheek that had put him on the right track and enabled him to provide Halliday with the evidence that he needed to bring the case to a successful conclusion.

It had been a big surprise to Halliday. He had never suspected that the dead woman was not Thelma but Jill and it was only the sight of the mole on Beatal's face that had raised that dormant memory in Tony's mind and led him to guess the truth.

He remembered that when he had first seen Jill Manners — the day she had come for the packet there had been no small mole beside her left eye. But there had been one on the second occasion he had seen her. It had only registered in his subconscious mind and it had taken the mole on Simon Beatal's face to bring it to the surface.

'Well, I'm hoping we've heard the last of it all,' said Andy. 'Maybe, now they've arrested the woman we'll have a peaceful season.'

'That goes for me too,' declared Billy fervently. 'I expected to find myself in clink any minute.'

'I don't think they ever really suspected you,' said Tony.

'They got near enough to be unpleasant,' declared Billy.

'Maybe this will teach ye to leave the girls alone in future,' said Andy severely. 'Ye see what they can turn out to be like.'

'There's something in that,' grinned Billy. 'Perhaps I'd better seriously think of going steady.'

'Vera's a very nice girl,' said Tony.

'Who said anything about Vera,' demanded Billy.

'I was thinking it was about time somebody did,' said Tony.

'Well, there's no denying she's attractive,' said Billy thoughtfully. 'She doesn't hit you all at once . . . '

'Aye, she grows on ye,' said Andy.

'Like Beryl?' suggested Billy.

'I'm seriously considering that matter,' said Andy to his surprise. 'She asked me to look after her Post Office savings book for her — and she's of the saving kind.'

'That was pretty cute of her,' said Billy. 'I've heard of 'say it with flowers' and 'say it with music' but a Post Office savings book is a new one.'

'Ye must admit it's practical,' said Andy.

'She won't be able to save much once she's got you to look after, poor girl,' said Billy.

'Maybe,' replied Andy. 'And then, of course, I'll no be able to pay her her full salary after we're married.'

'Why, you old robber,' said Tony.

'It'd cost me too much in income tax,' retorted Andy.

There was a tap at the door and Superintendent Halliday entered.

'I hope,' said Andy as he caught sight of him, 'that ye havena come to ask a lot of questions?'

'No, sir. I shan't be bothering you any more,' said Halliday cheerfully.

'Well, that's a relief,' declared Billy.

'I must say, Superintendent, there's a lot I dinna understand,' said Andy.

'It's very simple, sir,' said Halliday. 'Thelma Granger is a thorough bad lot, in my opinion. She was after the money from this uranium strike that her father had made. But he'd made a will before he went on his expedition leaving everything to Jill. He deposited this with a firm of lawyers in Šaskachewan. He told Granger about it in the letter he wrote when he was dying. Now you see why Thelma killed Jill?'

'To take her place,' said Billy.

'Exactly,' said Halliday. 'With *Thelma* apparently dead and *Jill* alive everything was easy. Granger could have registered the claim on her behalf and nobody could dispute it.'

'How did you get all this information?' asked Billy.

'Hargreaves told me a lot,' said Halliday. 'When he knew that Granger was dead. He didn't know it was Jill who had died. It was only Beatal who tumbled to that. Granger thought that Thelma was working in with him and that they would cash in together, but I believe she always intended to kill her husband when he was no longer useful. A real bad lot. Most of this scheme was hers. She thought up the business of the dummy packets so that they could ditch Hargreaves and Renton.'

'Which one threw the packet into our

compartment?' asked Billy. 'Jill, I suppose?'

'Yes, that was Jill. It was also Jill who came the first time to see Mr. Wayne. That wasn't part of the plan, you see. The arrangement was that Jill should bring the packet down to Hargreaves — she'd no idea what it was — and then go to the caravan and meet Thelma. The original idea was to kill her there and drop her body over the cliff and later identify her as Thelma. But when she told Thelma about throwing the packet into your compartment because she was scared of Beatal, and that she was going back to the Dome that evening to fetch it, Thelma thought of a better plan. She followed her. There was nobody here when Jill arrived, or when Thelma got here a few minutes later. She strangled Jill and put the body in the basket . . . '

'She took an awful risk,' said Andy.

'But she got away with it,' said Halliday. 'From then on she became Jill. I thought that story she told me in the caravan was wrong somewhere — all that business of changing clothes and the rest of it — it didn't ring true. I thought there was something queer about it, but I never guessed the real truth.'

'Why did she kill Gilbert — sorry, Howard?' asked Billy.

'He found out what the game was,' said Halliday. 'He discovered Jill's hat and it had got her name in it. He wasn't quite sure but he tackled Thelma about it and she spun him the same story she'd told me, about changing clothes. But he was still suspicious. She knew he hadn't any real proof but he was liable to be dangerous. She killed him while you were all at rehearsal.'

'I think it was very smart of you to get on to all this, Superintendent,' said Billy. 'I don't know how you did it?'

Superintendent Halliday almost blushed.

'I really shouldn't take any credit for it, sir,' he said. 'It was actually Mr. Wayne who discovered the truth.'

'Tony!' Billy grinned. 'Well, well, Anthony Wayne, the great detective!'

'I say we'll have to hurry,' said Andy. 'The show starts in two minutes. Get a move on will ye? Have ye been in front,

Superintendent?'

'No, sir, not yet,' said Halliday. 'I'd rather like to bring the wife this evening.'

'There'll be two seats waiting for ye in the box office,' said Andy. 'They'll no be the most expensive, ye understand?'

'Naturally, sir,' said Halliday gravely.

'Come on,' said Andy, 'we'll be off!'

They all trooped out into the passage. Sharon came hurriedly out of her dressing room.

'Oh,' she said as she caught sight of Halliday. 'Don't tell me there's more trouble?'

'No, miss,' he said, smiling. 'Its all over now — thanks to Mr. Wayne.'

'I didn't do much,' said Tony deprecatingly.

'You put us on the right track, sir,' said Halliday. 'Well, goodbye. I shall look forward to seeing your show tonight and thank you.'

He nodded and went out the stage door.

'What did you do?' asked Sharon curiously.

'Nothing very much,' said Tony.

'Only showed 'em who the murderer was,' said Billy. 'Good work, Sherlock.'

'It was that girl who was killed, wasn't it?' said Sharon. 'I shall never forget how scared she looked . . . '

'She had something to be scared about,' said Tony.

'Yes,' said Sharon. 'Poor girl . . . Oh, I forgot, I'm not speaking to you.'

'Couldn't you go on forgetting?' asked Tony.

'Well,' she looked up at him. 'Perhaps I might . . . '

Completely disregarding the rest of them, Tony caught her in his arms and kissed her.

THE END

We do hope that you have enjoyed reading this large print book.

Did you know that all of our titles are available for purchase?

We publish a wide range of high quality large print books including:
**Romances, Mysteries, Classics
General Fiction
Non Fiction and Westerns**

Special interest titles available in large print are:
**The Little Oxford Dictionary
Music Book, Song Book
Hymn Book, Service Book**

Also available from us courtesy of Oxford University Press:
**Young Readers' Dictionary
(large print edition)
Young Readers' Thesaurus
(large print edition)**

For further information or a free brochure, please contact us at:
**Ulverscroft Large Print Books Ltd.,
The Green, Bradgate Road, Anstey,
Leicester, LE7 7FU, England.
Tel:** (00 44) **0116 236 4325**
Fax: (00 44) **0116 234 0205**

**MURDER, MYSTERY
AND MAGIC**

John Burke

An innocent man is arrested for a murder committed by a woman . . . A guilty man confesses to another murder — but the police arrest an innocent woman! A man finds the woman of his dreams — and finds he's in a nightmare . . . The tenants of a new block of flats are so delighted with their new home that they don't really want to go out — little realizing that they *can't* leave. Strange incidents from macabre stories of *Murder, Mystery* . . . *and Magic*.

THE WAGER

E. C. Tubb

Captain Tom Mason of Homicide has a peculiarly horrible case to deal with. He investigates a murder where the victim has been decapitated. However, only the body remains at the crime scene. The murderer appears to have taken the head as a grisly trophy. Prompt police action, as they cordon off the area, yields four suspects. One of them, identified as running from the scene, is held in custody — but then another three people are decapitated . . .

THE WHITE FRIAR

Donald Stuart

Alexander Kielmann pursued his nefarious activities with impunity . . . blackmail, burglary, even murder. At Scotland Yard there were suspicions, but no proof available. Then Kielmann received a letter: *'You have ruined lives, but death is waiting for you . . . Your associates will suffer . . . They will receive their just deserts, you yourself being reserved for the last. I am Death, and I enclose my card.'* A visiting card showed a drawing of a monk in a white habit and cowl. Who was the *White Friar*?

CURTAIN CALL

Geraldine Ryan

It seemed too good an opportunity to miss . . . Impoverished by her father's death, Kate Spenser has been forced to give up music lessons, despite her talent. So when the enigmatic pianist John Hawksley comes to stay with her wealthy neighbours, Kate cannot resist asking him to teach her. She was not to know Hawksley's abrupt manner would cause friction between them, nor that the manipulative Euphemia would set out to ensnare the one man who seemed resistant to her charms . . .